CROSS PURPOSES

HENRY CECIL

Cross Purposes

London
MICHAEL JOSEPH

First published in Great Britain by
Michael Joseph Ltd
52 Bedford Square
London WC1B 3EF
1976

ISBN 0 7181 1442 6

Set and printed in Great Britain by
Tonbridge Printers Ltd, Peach Hall Works, Tonbridge, Kent
in Baskerville ten on twelve point on paper supplied by
P. F. Bingham Ltd, and bound by James Burn
at Esher, Surrey

CONTENTS

CHAPTER ONE

Strange Encounter

Shortly before the holding of the Referendum on the Common Market Douglas Barton was sitting in a window-seat with his back to the engine in one of the old-fashioned carriages which are still sometimes used on the route from Victoria to Redhill. He was holding the evening paper the right way up but not reading it. Douglas was well-educated and had been successful in his profession but, being a librarian and not a barrister, he had not been asked to give particulars of his career for inclusion in *Who's Who*. If the publishers of that dictionary had wished to include his name, his entry would have read something like this :

BARTON, Douglas Alexander, M.A. B.Litt : *b* 16 Oct. 1920 : *o s* of late Rev. Gilbert Barton and Mabel Barton (née Bilsby); *m* 1945 Sheila Maud, *y d* of late Arthur Carrington; one *s* two *d*. Educ : St Andrew's Coll., Lincoln; King's Coll., Cambridge. Chief Librarian New British Fiction Library, 1968–. *Recreation* : listening to music. *Address* : Old Cottage, Sycamore Lane, Redhill, Surrey.

It would be a pleasant, if impracticable, idea for *Who's Who* to obtain and publish an objective assessment of the characters of those whose names are included in it. '*p a.*' – the abbreviation for 'pompous ass' – at the end of a full column of achievements would add to the readability of the book. And the risk of collecting such a comment might limit the number of those who write despairing letters to the publishers year after year suggesting that surely it was time that their names were included.

Such an entry in Douglas's case would have stated (in an abbreviated form) that he was a good-humoured, tolerant, modest man of considerable ability but without sufficient ambition to make a mark in the world.

He had been chosen out of three hundred applicants to be the first Chief Librarian of the new British Fiction Library. The object of the founders of this library was to include in it, as far as was humanly possible, every work of fiction written in English (whether a translation or not) from the Apocrypha onwards. When necessary it would arrange for a book to be reprinted and, after the Library had been in existence for two years, it offered a free subscription as a prize to anyone who could point out five books which were not included in its catalogue. The salary attached to Douglas's position was substantially less than that of an experienced compositor, namely £5,000 a year. It was mainly because of this salary that Douglas was not reading his paper. His twin daughters, aged fifteen, were very happily at school, but the fees were high and the difficulties of keeping them there and of enabling them to go on to a university when they had finished school were a source of great worry to Douglas and his wife. Every month their standard of living had dropped and they had had to economise in almost every way, except where such economies might affect the girls' education or the health of the family. No longer did Douglas's car await him at Redhill station, but, provided it had not been stolen, he would make the journey from the train to his home in Sycamore Lane on a bicycle. He was wondering what else they could give up when he was interrupted in these depressing thoughts by a question from the man sitting opposite, whom up to that moment he had hardly noticed.

'Excuse me, sir, would you mind if I opened the window?'

'Certainly not. I should enjoy the air.'

'Might I ask you a very rude question, sir?'

Douglas's answer to the first question was almost automatic, for he was still concentrating on the problem of how to find the next term's school fees. But the second question jolted him out of these reflections, and, although perhaps he did not realise it, he was grateful for its unexpected nature.

'I don't mind,' he said.

'Thank you, sir. It's nothing very terrible really. I simply wondered why you hadn't opened the window yourself if you wanted some fresh air.'

'Frankly, I hadn't thought of it.'

'Absorbed in the paper, I suppose?'

'As a matter of fact I wasn't.'

'Perhaps you were wondering how to vote about the Common Market?'

Many people would have snubbed the man and retired into their papers or their thoughts, but Douglas was pleased to be interrupted and was a little intrigued to know how the conversation would continue. The stranger was fairly well dressed, and had an intelligent face and lips which suggested that he smiled a good deal.

'No,' said Douglas, 'I made up my mind about that months ago.'

'An economist perhaps?'

'No, I'm not. In point of fact I haven't the faintest idea whether it would be a good or a bad thing for the country. I suspect I am in the same position as 99 per cent of the voters. We have wholly insufficient information upon which to form a worthwhile view. I am relying solely on the views of a few friends of mine who appear to know a good deal about the subject.'

'Then the chances are that you're voting to stay in. No, I don't expect an answer,' said the stranger hurriedly. 'I believe

9

in the secrecy of the ballot.'

'You haven't yet opened the window,' said Douglas.

'Thank you. I will. As you may have guessed, I only asked the question in order to get into conversation with you. I haven't spoken to an educated man for well over two years – unless you count the prison chaplain. I only came out today. Don't be alarmed,' he added, 'it wasn't for violence.'

Douglas and his wife had differing views about crime and punishment. His were conservative. Although he was averagely compassionate he considered that prison and punishment were necessary evils and that some harm was done by those who pressured the Government to release prisoners before they had paid the penalty. He thought that punishment was a good thing, both as a deterrent to others and as a method of satisfying the public's desire for redress against those who had broken the law. Sheila thought very differently. She believed that, although it was a natural instinct for people to want revenge on a person who had committed a crime, it was an instinct which should be repressed in a Christian country. She was one of those who were in favour of the movement to abolish prison altogether, except for the purpose of protecting the public from violent people. Prison is a comparatively new institution. Until nearly the end of the 18th century criminals were treated in a much more economic way. They were either executed or transported. Today it must cost a hundred million pounds a year or more to keep people in prison, and the public can ill afford it.

'Fraud was my line, though I once tried a burglary to see what it was like. I can tell you I was terrified out of my wits. That little girl in Angus Wilson's story *Late Call* was quite right when she said, "How awful to be big and to be afraid". Fraud's quite different. It's rather fun, as a matter of fact, particularly as you don't feel sorry for your victims. But I was sorry for the old lady whose house I burgled. She was nearly as frightened as I was. But some of the people I used to cheat wanted something for nothing. And the fun was that I got it and they didn't. As you're no doubt a respectable citizen, you'll be sorry to hear that I've got three thousand pounds waiting for me in a safe deposit to start my new life.'

'More fraud?' asked Douglas.

'As a matter of fact, no. I'm going to go straight. I know a lot of people say that when they come out of prison and it's quite true that most first offenders don't come back for more. But that isn't because they're reformed or rehabilitated. It's because they hated it in prison so much that they don't want another dose. Their characters are exactly the same. You can't change your character, though you can change your way of life. I've decided to go straight but not because I'm a better man. Like most people I'm dishonest by nature. The average person subdues that side of his nature because it pays him to do so. Where do you live, by the way?'

'I get out at Redhill.'

'So do I. But that doesn't tell you where I live. And d'you know why I want to go straight?'

'Please tell me if you would like to.'

'As a matter of fact, it's because of the smell. I love fresh clean air and the smell in nearly every prison is perfectly appalling. I'm surprised I didn't give up the game after my first term. The truth was that I didn't know how to do it.'

'How are you going to do it, may I ask?'

'Fair question. It's extremely difficult. It's not simply the problem of getting a job. Oddly enough that's easier than you might expect. The difficulty is to find some way of compelling oneself to restrain one's natural instincts. And there is only one way to do it.' He waited for Douglas to ask him what that way was but, when he didn't, he went on : 'To get married. But that's not going to be easy, is it? And that's a question I'd like to ask you. Should I tell the girl my past history as soon as I meet her or should I wait until I see a relationship beginning?'

'I've never thought about it,' said Douglas.

'Well, you'd be doing an ex-con man a favour on his first day out of prison by giving him the benefit of your advice – until we reach Redhill of course. I suppose you wouldn't like to give me a lift to the local hotel?'

'I'm afraid I can't. I'm riding a bicycle.'

'I thought only Lord Hailsham did that. The price of petrol, I suppose. It's also good exercise. But on a wild wet windy evening I'd prefer to forgo the exercise.'

'My wife usually meets me when that happens.'

'Let's hope it rains tonight. Then you can give me a lift. Or would your wife object?'

'As a matter of fact,' said Douglas, 'I don't think she would.'

'Is she a prison visitor or something?'

'Not exactly.'

'Any children?'

'Two girls and a boy.'

'You must be a happy man.'

'Yes.'

'I'd give a lot to be in your position.'

'I hope you will be one day.'

'The difficulty is to start.'

'Haven't you any relatives or friends?'

'None that would help. Most of my friends are in the same line of business as I was. And my relatives haven't wanted to know for a long time. My present name is Edward Livermore, by the way. But you haven't answered my question. If I tell a girl as soon as I meet her, she probably won't want to know me any more. And, if I don't, she'll say I've been deceiving her. And that to some extent will be true. What d'you advise me to do?'

After a little thought Douglas said : 'On the whole I think that it pays to tell the truth.'

'Not when your wife asks you if you think she's looking any slimmer.'

'I said "on the whole", and I'm not referring to the sort of lie that everyone has to tell from time to time.'

'But why should a girl have anything to do with a man who has been to prison four or five times?'

'Some girls might want to help you.'

'I'm not sure that that's the sort of girl I'd like to marry. And wouldn't any girl think about the children? Aren't my children likely to take after me? Surely there's a good chance that they will. Good gracious. I quite forgot. I've got a thousand pounds in premium bonds.'

'What work d'you expect to do, may I ask?'

'I'm not sure really. But I can always get a job as a garage mechanic. That's something I do really know something about. Your car doesn't need a rebore, I suppose?'

'No, thank you very much.'

'May I ask what you do for a living? I won't apologise each time for being impertinent.'

'I'm a librarian.'

'Good gracious. I'm not surprised you go home by bicycle. You can't get much out of that. More than I got at the Scrubs, I suppose. How d'you manage to bring up a family on what you get?'

'I'm afraid that's my business.'

'Of course it is. D'you have to pay school fees?'

'I hope you don't think I've been unfriendly,' said Douglas, 'but there really is a limit.'

'There's no need to apologise, I assure you. I think you've been particularly nice. What d'you reckon it costs to keep a person in food these days? As one of a family I mean.'

'It's going up all the time. It's certainly gone up a fantastic amount in the last two years.'

'Would ten pounds a week do it, d'you think?'

'I suppose it might.'

'You don't happen to have a spare room, I suppose?'

'Not at the moment.'

'D'you know,' said Edward, 'I'd pay a thousand pounds – in advance – if you'd let me live with you for six months and introduce me to your friends.'

'Quite impossible, I'm afraid.'

'You may not want to do it. You may not agree to do it. But I'm sure it's not impossible. That spare room I referred to was only not available because you saw what was coming and it wasn't going to be available for me. So it could be done and, if I stayed with you for six months – that's twenty-six weeks – say, two hundred and sixty pounds for my keep – that would give you £750 for school fees. That would be a help, wouldn't it? You might be able to use the car even when it wasn't raining.'

'I'm sorry,' said Douglas, 'it's quite out of the question.'

'Why? Because I'm a complete stranger or because I've been a con man?'

'Both, I'm afraid. Look at it from my point of view. Just imagine you were a married man with a family. You meet someone on the train and you go home and say to your wife : "This is Mr Livermore. I met him on the train and he's going to stay here for six months. By the way, he's just come out of prison where he's been several times." Wouldn't your wife think that you'd lost your senses?'

'Never having been married, I couldn't rightly say, but I expect she would think it a bit odd, if I did it like that. How about your bringing her to meet me at the pub where I'll be staying? You could come to dinner. That won't bind you to anything and, if your wife took a liking to me, we might do a deal. What harm could that do? All you've got to say to your wife is "I met quite a nice chap on the train. We had an interesting conversation and I've given him our telephone number. He may ring us up to ask us for a drink." You needn't say anything about Wormwood Scrubs at that stage. You can do all that before you ask me to stay with you. What's wrong with the idea?'

'Quite out of the question.'

'But suppose I hadn't just come out of prison and was an ordinary chap you met on the train and you'd enjoyed talking to me? Your wife wouldn't think it odd then, would she?'

'Perhaps not. But that isn't the case. You tell me yourself you've been living on the proceeds of fraud. How am I to know if there's any truth in what you've said to me?'

'You mean I might have been lying when I said I'd been to prison?'

'Well, yes, that's possible too. You may be a practical joker.'

'They don't do much harm.'

'Maybe not. But my wife wouldn't thank me for striking up an acquaintance with one.'

'But in fact you do believe that I've been to prison, don't you?'

'Yes, I suppose I do.'

'But what you say is that you've no reason to believe that I'm going straight in the future. That's true. Nor have you any reason to believe that I've got three thousand pounds in a safe deposit and a thousand premium bonds.'

'I'm not concerned with that.'

'But you would be, if I were going to pay you a thousand pounds in advance. Tell you what. If I send you a hundred ten pound notes by registered post, which you can give back to me if nothing comes of our suggestion, would you and your wife come to dinner with me?'

'Certainly not.'

'How much do you want?'

'I don't want anything, I'm afraid,' said Douglas. 'It's certainly been an experience talking to you and I hope that you'll succeed in going straight and getting married and—'

'And that I'll live happily ever after.'

'Yes, certainly.'

'But you won't do anything to assist me in the process?'

'I'm afraid not.'

'Why shouldn't you?'

'Why should I?'

'That's simply answered. A thousand pounds. It would be quite useful, you know.'

'I've nothing further to say on the subject.'

'Well, at least tell me your name and where you live.'

'I'm afraid not.'

'But you have told me.'

'What d'you mean by that?'

'Well, you've only got a bicycle, haven't you, at the station and I didn't tell you that I used to be quite a good cross-country runner. If you won't give me your name and address I could run after you. In the bad old days men used to run from stations to help people with their luggage. Sometimes they'd run several miles in order to get a shilling. And they weren't cross-country runners. So it's up to you, isn't it?'

Douglas said nothing. 'I shall enjoy a run,' said Edward.

'I shall ask the police to stop you from molesting me.'

'But I shan't be molesting you. I shall be running behind you at a respectful distance and not throwing things at you or calling you names and, as soon as I've seen the house you go into, I shall just take its name and go away again. It's not against the law, is it? You're not a violent man, I take it? You wouldn't try and hit me on the nose or anything of that sort?'

'No.'

'Then it couldn't be called conduct likely to cause a breach of the peace, could it? Because I'm not going to break the peace. And you said you weren't. And a policeman can come too on a bicycle, if you like, to see fair play. So wouldn't it save a lot of trouble if you just gave me your name and address?'

'I'm getting a little tired of this,' said Douglas. 'I can see that I can't stop you from learning where we live, but I can assure you that, if you write to us, your letters will not be answered and, if you telephone, we will hang up the receiver as soon as we know who it is.'

'And that's the way you treat a poor chap who's just come out of prison and who's told you that he wants to go straight and has got no relatives or friends in the world. It's just an encouragement to me to go on with crime. I can't think why you won't give me a chance. You can find out from the police, if you want to, that I'm not a violent man. Aren't you supposed to help me back into society? Isn't that the duty of Christian men and women? Or perhaps you and your wife aren't?'

'Mr Whatever-your-name-is,' said Douglas, 'I'm afraid I should prefer to end this conversation.'

'Oh well,' said Edward, 'there was no harm in trying. Now just have a look at this.' He put his hand into one of his pockets and brought out a roll of ten-pound notes. 'There should be fifty,' he said. 'I didn't count them. I took the Bank's word.' He put his hand into another pocket and brought out another roll of notes. This time they were fivers. 'There are supposed to be fifty of these too,' he said. 'D'you know there was a time when I wouldn't carry fivers about with me at all. When they first came out, I used two of them as though they were pound notes. After that I wouldn't have them. Till now of course. They're only worth what a pound used to be. I suppose you think,' he said, 'that these are the proceeds of my last swindle. Well, they aren't,' he went on, 'they're only part of the proceeds.'

The average honest person, like Douglas, has never held a lot of cash in his hand. Probably the most that Douglas had ever possessed in cash was about a hundred pounds. That was many years previously when it represented the deposit on a car. £750 would be extremely useful to him at the moment. And, if he had thought about it, he would have had to admit to himself that he was distracted by the sight of the money at a time when he was worried as to how he was going to find the next term's school fees, the rates, the interest on his mortgage and the insurance premiums payable to BUPA and the motor insurance company. He had a certain wistful longing to be the possessor of this money.

'This represents part of the proceeds of a bit of kite-flying,' said Edward. 'D'you happen to know what that is?'

'Isn't it something to do with robbing a bank?'

'Quite right. It's the gentlemanly way to rob a bank. No masks, no revolvers, nobody hurt except the feelings of a bank manager. Would you like to know how it's done?'

'No,' lied Douglas. He would have liked to know, simply as a matter of interest. Certainly not for the purpose of doing it himself.

'Well, I'll tell you,' said Edward. 'It may help to convince you that I really am an old lag in need of redemption. I once heard kite-flying called the art of borrowing money from a bank which is not prepared to lend it to you. Any number of persons can play this game, but I prefer to play it by myself. For several reasons. First, there's nobody to share the loot with and secondly there's nobody to give the game away except yourself. Well, it's done like this. You open an account with a bank. Even I with all my previous convictions can do that. I could even do it in my real name, but I don't think I'd try that unless I were going straight. The day may come when by the use of computers and various other electronic devices it may become impossible to conceal who you really are. But at the moment I'm glad to say – or, rather, if I weren't going straight, I'd be glad to say – that there are a good number of agencies and pressure groups which are doing all they can to make life easier for the criminal by helping him to conceal his identity and by preventing people from prying into his various non-social practices. I have never been able to understand why that sort of thing gets such public support. If I were an honest man – or should I say when I'm an honest man – I wouldn't mind the police coming in to inspect my books and all my property. I shouldn't mind accountants looking at my banking accounts and all that sort of thing. People call it snooping, but what's wrong with snooping if there's something illegal to conceal? And how does it hurt you, if there isn't? There are, of course, international industrial spies who indulge in practices designed to hurt the State or some competitor in their line of business. But, as far as the State's concerned, it's up to it to defeat that sort of thing by counter-espionage. As far as ordinary private business is concerned, it's up to them to look after themselves.

'But I'm straying from the subject. How to borrow money from a bank which is not prepared to lend it to you. If I walked into a bank where I had £3.04 in my account and no security and asked them to lend me £500 they would of course refuse, but, if I offered them a cheque made payable to me on another bank, they would very likely advance me some of the proceeds of that cheque before they had cleared it. So all I do is to open another account with another bank in another name and, as Donald Somebody-or-Other, I draw a cheque in favour of Edward Livermore for five hundred pounds. Suppose the bank lets me have, say, a hundred and fifty against this cheque, I put it on a horse or a politician. If I win, I've got the money to put into the second bank to enable the cheque for five hundred pounds to be honoured. If I lose, all I do is to go through the converse process. As Edward Livermore I draw a cheque for, say, a thousand pounds and put it into Donald Somebody-or-Other's account at the second bank. This enables them to clear the first cheque for five hundred and to give me, say, two fifty to put on the next horse. Have you followed so far?'

'As much as I want to.'

'Quite so. An amusing way is to have an account at all five banks, provided you remember which name you have to sign for which account. Of course, if your horses always run too slowly or your politicians never get enough votes, eventually the balloon will go up. And that's when you scarper. Fortunately I put some of the loot in a safe deposit. But they were too quick for me at the airport. I was a cross-country runner, not a sprinter. By the way, would a few of these be of any use to you?' He indicated the ten-pound notes. They would have been of considerable use to Douglas, but he did not say so.

'If the bank that lost the money knew that you had these notes, couldn't they sue you for them?'

'Certainly they could. If they knew I'd got them and where. Yes, if you chose to ring up the bank in question and say that you'd met me and that you'd seen that I'd got in my possession £750 which I had stated was part of the proceeds of my last crime, they could come after me for it. But they wouldn't find it, you know. They'd make me bankrupt, but that doesn't help them to find the money.'

'If you're really going straight,' said Douglas, 'surely the first thing for you to do to show your good faith is to give back to the bank which you've robbed as much money as you can.'

'Strictly speaking you're right,' said Edward, 'but I think that would be carrying things a bit far. You see I've done my three years.'

'That doesn't give you a right to the money.'

'No, I suppose not, but, if I use the money sensibly, I'll probably be able to become a respectable law-abiding citizen. If I gave it all back, I might be tempted out of necessity to fall back on my old practices.'

'I thought you said you could get a job as a garage mechanic. That would give you enough to live on without stealing money from other people.'

'Quite true,' said Edward. 'Maybe I shall start that way, but that would be with a view to acquiring my own business. You see, for many years I have been used to a certain standard of living which, except when I'm in prison, I try to maintain. It costs the country about forty pounds a week or more to keep a man in prison. I may live, say, another thirty years or so. If I spend fifteen of those years in prison it will cost you and your fellow citizens some £30,000. Probably a good deal more in view of inflation. The bank can easily spare the £3,000 that I've got. It's written off as lost, I've no doubt. Wouldn't it be better from every point of view to use it to keep me out of prison? If only from the point of view of the economy of the country?'

'That may be so,' said Douglas. 'But it's no good your pretending to yourself that you're going straight if you start off that process by spending money which doesn't belong to you instead of giving it back to the true owner.'

'Oh it's easy to be good on £5,000 a year.'

'How on earth did you know?' asked Douglas.

'There are some criminals who are quite literate, you know,' said Edward. 'Isn't that what Becky Sharp said?'

'I'm sorry.' When Edward had mentioned five thousand pounds, Douglas was so struck by the fact that that was his actual salary that for the moment he did not appreciate the allusion to *Vanity Fair*.

'Five thousand a year in Becky Sharp's day,' went on Edward, 'would be worth about fifty thousand or more now. In fact much more. You really can't compare them. In those days income tax took away nothing at all. Today it takes away most of it. I'd better pocket these now,' he added. 'Sure I can't interest you in my samples?'

Douglas did not answer. He picked up his paper again, still the right way up, and this time he actually read a paragraph, though he had not the faintest idea what it said.

'If only,' he was thinking, 'Sheila could win one of her football pools.' The sight of the money was disturbing. Edward must have realised this because he was very slow in putting it back into his pocket.

'D'you know,' said Edward, 'I came to Victoria by underground.'

'That was pretty risky with all these pickpockets about.'

'I know, but I like the feel of it. I know there's a risk of

21

being mugged but at the moment there's only one person who knows I've got all this money on me besides me. And that's you. And I'll tell you this. If I were mugged on the way out of Redhill station I should be quite certain it wasn't you. I wonder if you've ever done anything dishonest. I tell you an idea I've had. Some years ago I was going by underground and I put a penny in a tuppenny slot machine and the ticket came out before I had put the other penny in. Oddly enough I'm honest in small ways. It's pounds that I steal, not pence. So, without thinking, I put the other penny in. Then I realised I'd created the same problem for the next traveller. It seems to me it would be quite a good idea to start off the machine with a coin and then to watch what happens, putting in another whenever the traveller accepted his good luck. Of course you could never really be sure, because when he got home the conscientious man might send the extra money to the railway. But I doubt if many people would do that.' The train began to slow down. 'This must be Redhill. I'm sorry I can't interest you in my welfare, but, if you change your mind about me when you've told your wife all about this conversation, I'll tell you where you can get hold of me. I shall go to the nearest and best country house hotel that I can find. You must know where that is. If you ask for me under the name of Edward Livermore I shall be only too delighted to renew our acquaintance. By the way, I'm not going to follow you. I shall leave the ball firmly in your court. Don't forget. A thousand pounds for six months. And you can see for yourself that I've got the best part of it on me.'

Not long afterwards the train drew into Redhill and they both got out. It was not raining, Douglas's bicycle was still there and he was soon on his way home.

Meanwhile, Edward sought the stationmaster, made a few enquiries from him and then took a taxi to Holly Towers.

CHAPTER TWO

Ends Hardly Meet

Douglas Barton was a lucky man in most respects. He had the right wife, the right children, the right house, the right job and, indeed, almost everything except the right money.

Sheila was good-looking, good-tempered and a good cook. She and Douglas would have been very happy together alone. But they both enjoyed family life and only one of their children was grown up. This was Theodore, who was twenty-two. He was quite different from the rest of the family. They were interested to a greater or a lesser degree in the arts. Music and painting meant nothing to him and he read very little except upon his own subjects. He was the only scientific member of a classical family. His subjects were wireless and electronics. He refused to go to a university but studied both his subjects at the nearest polytechnic. He then started up his own business in a shed at the bottom of the garden. He began in a very small way with a couple of hundred pounds capital, which he had saved from his earnings as a washer-upper in pubs and hotels during the school holidays. His first commercial venture was to make parts for electronic instruments and wireless sets. At the same time he was carrying on with his greater interest, which was inventing. At the age of eighteen he built himself a model aeroplane which would fly and which he could control by the use of a wireless transmitter which he had also constructed. At first he made himself rather unpopular at home, because the buzzing of the aeroplane round the garden at any time of day or night sometimes got on his parents' nerves, particularly at night. Eventually he was persuaded to fly it half a mile away over the common, with the advantage from his point of view that he could keep the aeroplane in sight all the time, so that it was less likely to have a crash. On several occasions while flying it near his own home it had run into a chimney pot or a garden wall or some other obstruction and on one occasion it was so badly damaged that he had had to start again from scratch.

While his parents admired his skill and inventiveness, they did not understand any of the technicalities and they used to profess a lively interest which they did not feel. So that when he announced proudly one day that he could control the aeroplane from a distance of nearly a quarter of a mile away, while they said the right things, they did not feel much enthusiasm when Theodore offered to explain how he had been able to increase the range.

The boy was not depressed by his parents' comparative lack of interest. He was an inventor and his reward came from the knowledge that some of his inventions worked. By the time he was twenty-two he had built up a small business and was earning about a thousand a year. It was a very small income but he was determined not to make the mistake which the owners of so many small businesses are inclined to make when they smell success and become too ambitious. They borrow too much money from the bank to increase their turnover and then find that, if things go wrong, there is nothing for it but to close down and start again, with a period of bankruptcy in the middle. Moreover, he only spent half his time on the conduct and improvement of his business. The other half he spent in inventing. The second half of the 20th century is probably the most satisfactory period in history for a small inventor. This is because, while it cannot truthfully be said that now everything is possible, it is not difficult to believe that almost nothing is impossible. So Theodore was a very happy young man, living in an atmosphere of excitement and with attainment always on the horizon.

His sisters were twins, very much alike in looks, in thoughts and habits. They were fifteen and at boarding school and they enjoyed it there, particularly as they shared their father's fondness for music and considerable emphasis was placed by the school on this subject. They loved their parents and they had no particular ambitions in life except to marry and to be as happy as Mum and Dad.

So the whole family enjoyed life, and this was no doubt partly because Douglas and Sheila were determined to do all they could for their children. It was this determination that made Douglas have a more uncomfortable ride home from the station than usual. He knew that the problem facing him was no greater than that which faced many middle-class families in the 1970s. Although he was fond of good food and drink he did not so much mind the reduction in their living standards, provided that they had sufficient satisfactory food to eat. But as he cycled home, he couldn't help comparing their situation with that of the man in the train. Without any unjustifiable extravagance, they found themselves each week coming nearer to the day when they simply would not have enough money to pay for their girls' education. Whereas the criminal or ex-criminal had seven hundred and fifty pounds in cash in his pocket and probably over three thousand as well in a safe deposit or in premium bonds. And he would pay no tax on any of it. Nevertheless Douglas never seriously considered Edward's coming to stay with them as a feasible suggestion, even though it would bring in a thousand pounds.

Much as he would have liked £750, the idea of introducing a criminal stranger into his family was absolutely ludicrous. It could not be considered for a moment, could it? Edward had offered to put £1,000 into the post, and having regard to what

Douglas had seen, it was almost certain that he would be able to do this and quite possible that he would actually do it. But then the man was either mad or bad or both. If they were to be reduced to taking in paying guests, they were not going to start with a man who, whether he had robbed banks or not, talked about such crimes as though they hardly mattered at all. But he'd never considered paying guests before. That was a possibility. By the time he had begun to work out how much they could charge, he had arrived home. He put his bicycle away and then opened the front door where his wife was waiting for him. The first thing she said after they had kissed each other was, 'Sherry's gone up, I'm afraid.'

'Even that Cyprus stuff?'

'Yes. I thought we'd try some of this.' She indicated a bottle of British sherry.

'Oh God, has it come to that? Perhaps we'd better cut it out altogether.'

'Try it. After all it is alcoholic.'

He took a sip and made a wry face. 'So is methylated spirits.'

'We might get used to it.'

'I hope not. What sort of a day have you had?'

'Quite pleasant, but one thing I'm a bit worried about.'

'Oh dear. What is it?'

'Theo asked me if I thought you could let him have a hundred pounds.'

'Oh Lord. What's he want it for?'

'He says it isn't vital but he's a bit short at the moment, and it would be a help.'

'I'd like to let him have it, I must say. It's the first time he's asked for anything. I hope things are all right.'

'I asked him that and he said, "Oh yes." It's simply that cash is a bit short and he wants some materials.'

'D'you know how long he wants it for? I shall have to overdraw to get it and that will cost me twelve per cent or something like it.'

'He thought two or three months.'

'Hell,' said Douglas. 'D'you know, a man I met in the train produced £750 in cash.'

'What on earth d'you mean? Why did he do it?'

Douglas told her about his meeting with Edward.

'What an extraordinary man. D'you think he was telling you the truth?'

'I don't know. I expect some of it was true. How would you like to have him here for six months?'

'No, thank you very much,' said Sheila.

'Even with his thousand pounds?'

'Even with his thousand pounds.'

'But what about all this rehabilitation stuff you're so keen on?'

Sheila said nothing for a moment. 'That's a fair point,' she said eventually. 'The truth is, I suppose, that we're all in favour of other people doing the rehabilitation. When they want to put an open prison on our doorstep we have protest meetings.'

'You don't mean there is a scheme for one?'

'Oh no. I was just giving an example of the sort of thing that happens. I hope I'd be strong enough not to protest. It's terribly important that these people should be taken back into society.'

'Then what about Mr Wilberforce?'

'Wilberforce?'

'Whatever his name is. Livermore. The chap I met.'

'I simply couldn't bear it,' said Sheila.

'Nor could I.'

'Then why should anybody else? I'm rather glad this has happened really. It shows up the nakedness of the land. I'm sure Lord Longford would take in at least half a dozen ex-criminals into his house.'

'He probably has already.'

'I wonder how many other members of anti-prison Committees would do it.'

'If they agreed themselves,' said Douglas, 'their wives probably wouldn't. In point of fact in this case you're just as bad as I am. Strictly speaking, you ought to be saying that we ought to give the fellow a chance.'

'How can we? With the girls home for the holidays. He may be a sex-offender.'

'I could find out about that.'

'It's this thousand pounds that's affecting you, isn't it?'

'Of course it is. I wouldn't have considered the idea otherwise. I don't really consider it now. If you hadn't mentioned about Theo wanting a hundred pounds—'

'D'you think he'd be clean about the house?'

'He'd probably pinch the candlesticks.'

'I thought you were going to sell them.'

'I would have, only we can't get enough.'

'If you really wanted Theo to have the hundred pounds I could pop my engagement ring.'

'I wouldn't hear of it. I can get an overdraft, though it is a damn nuisance at the moment.'

At that moment Theodore came in. 'Hullo, Dad,' he said, 'had a good day?'

'Same as usual,' said Douglas. 'I hear you could do with a hundred pounds.'

'Only if it isn't inconvenient.'

'Oh no, that's perfectly all right. Any idea how long you want it for?'

'Now, Dad, be truthful about this. If I really needed it badly I'd say so. I can manage without it. But it would be quite useful.'

'I tell you, I can let you have it quite easily.'

'But then you asked how long I wanted it for.'

'I just wondered.'

'The fact is that I've seen an advertisement for some special screws going cheap.'

'It's not a mail order firm?'

'They're absolutely respectable but they want the cash with the order. Obviously trying to unload some stuff that they don't much want and it's just what I need. They're offering it for half last month's price. I expect it will be double in a couple of months. So you see it's really quite a good investment. They're not absolutely essential to me at the moment.'

'But these special screws will be essential to you in due course?'

'Oh yes. I use a lot of them. But I've enough to go on with.'

'I'll give you a cheque in the morning,' said Douglas.

'Sure it's all right?'

'Of course it's all right.'

'Thank you ever so much, Dad. By the way I think I'm on to something big.'

'D'you mean an invention?'

'Very much so.'

'What will it do?'

'You know the man who invented cats'-eyes made a fortune. If I succeed, I'll make another.'

'It's for the roads, is it?'

'Yes. I won't say any more at the moment, in case it doesn't come off.'

'That isn't the thing you want the screws for?'

'Oh no. They're just run of the mill stuff.'

'If your invention comes off,' said Sheila, 'how long d'you think it will be before you're in the money?'

'Oh good gracious, Mum, I haven't the faintest idea. If I'm on the right lines, I suppose I might finish it within about six months and then I'd have to sell it and that would probably take another six or nine months. With any reasonable luck we'll be celebrating it within a couple of years.'

'So we'll have to go on drinking British sherry for a couple of years, shall we?'

'Is it as bad as that?' said Theodore. 'Can I try a glass?'
Douglas poured some out, gave it to him, and raised his own

glass. 'Well, here's to the new invention. What will it do, by the way?'

'I think I'll wait till it's gone a bit farther before I tell you. Oh, by the way, have you done your football pools this week, Mum?'

'I haven't, as a matter of fact.'

'How long have you been doing them?'

'A couple of years and not a penny to show for it.'

'How do you fill them in? Form or what?'

'Mostly birthdays,' said Sheila.

'Let me try them for a week or two,' said Theodore. 'Perhaps I'll bring you luck.'

'All right. But I expect your invention will bring in the money long before the pools do.'

Theodore finished his sherry. 'I must get back now,' he said. 'Give me the coupons tomorrow.'

As soon as he'd gone out of the room Douglas said 'I notice you didn't say anything to him about our taking in a paying guest.'

'Of course not. Just when he wanted to borrow a hundred pounds. He wouldn't have taken it. He was pretty suspicious that you weren't really able to afford to lend it to him.'

'We couldn't have this chap, I suppose?' said Douglas.

'It's quite out of the question. I couldn't bear it. I mean, we'd have him at meals. We'd have no privacy at all, apart from the danger that he might walk off with something or that the police might come round here making enquiries. He'd probably start using your name and run up accounts and that sort of thing.'

'Your instincts are absolutely right. It's just not on.'

'I might ask one or two of the members of my committee if they can think of anybody.'

'I shouldn't do that,' said Douglas. 'The only reason I thought of it was because there was this thousand pounds. If you ask one of them he'll get it and not us and then we'd feel responsible when he let them down and waltzed off with everything. It is odd, though, that, just when I would like to lay my hands on about £750, the chap in the train should bring it out and dangle it in front of my eyes.'

At that moment there was a ring at the bell. 'Good gracious,' said Douglas, 'I suppose he hasn't followed me here after all.'

'I'll go and get rid of him,' said Sheila. She went to the door and opened it. It was Henry Bunting, a neighbour, whom they knew between themselves as Scrounging Henry. 'Do come in,' she said. 'How nice to see you.'

'I'm a bit late,' said the visitor. 'You said six o'clock, didn't you, and now it's nearly seven.'

Sheila hadn't in fact said anything. But whether it was a genuine mistake on his part or whether he was looking for a drink she would never know.

'Here's Henry,' she called out.

'Hell,' said Douglas to himself, 'what does he want now?'

'How nice to see you,' he said as they came in. 'Sit down and have a glass of sherry.

'I'm afraid I'm a bit late,' said Henry. 'I believe you said six o'clock and now it's nearly seven.'

'We were just going to ring you up,' said Douglas. He poured out a glass of sherry and handed it to Henry.

'Cheers,' said Henry. He took a fairly liberal drink and put his glass down. 'This isn't your usual sherry,' he said.

'It's going to be,' said Douglas. 'D'you like it?'

'What's it called?'

'Now, Henry,' said Sheila, 'you must tell us whether you like it before you know what it is.'

'Quite frankly I don't like it as much as the stuff you gave me the other night. As a matter of fact I was wondering whether you could lend me a bottle. I forgot to bring any home.'

'You're very welcome to have the remains of this one,' said Douglas.

'You're very kind,' said Henry doubtfully.

31

'Think nothing of it,' said Douglas. 'I'm sure you'd do the same for us if we were short.'

'I'm afraid we haven't got any blotting paper,' said Sheila.

'You haven't a crisp, I suppose?' said Henry.

'Not even that, I'm afraid. Are you hungry?'

'As a matter of fact, I am.'

'You'll be having dinner soon, won't you?' said Douglas.

'That's very kind of you,' said Henry. 'I'd no intention of coming to dinner, but if you press me, I'll yield.'

'I'm terribly sorry,' said Sheila. 'Douglas meant that you'd be having dinner at your home. I have to confess that there simply isn't enough to go round.'

'I'm not a very good trencherman,' said Henry, 'but I'd hate to make you go short.'

'We don't so much mind about ourselves,' said Sheila, 'but we've got Theo at home and he's got a good appetite and it's important to feed young people properly.'

'Of course it is,' said Henry. 'He's a nice young man, your Theo. He'll do well, I'm sure. I suppose you haven't such a thing as a bar of chocolate?'

'I'm afraid not,' said Douglas.

'You always used to have some around,' said Henry.

'We've given it up,' said Sheila. 'Part of the economy drive.'

'I don't know what it will come to next,' said Henry. 'Wherever you go, people are stopping that and knocking off this. I suppose next you'll be telling me you won't be able to lend me the Sunday papers that I don't take myself.'

'I have to read those,' said Douglas, 'for the book reviews. It's one of the things we can't give up.'

'Good,' said Henry. 'I'm giving up the *Sunday Times* and *Observer*. Perhaps you could let me have those when you've finished with them.'

'If you wouldn't mind calling for them on the Monday,' said Douglas, 'we should have read all we want by then.'

'Of course not. That will be fine. As a matter of fact, I do rather like reading them in bed on Sunday night. You couldn't stretch a point, I suppose? I tell you what. You keep the *Observer* and let me have the *Sunday Times*.'

Sheila decided to make an abrupt change in the conversation. 'Henry, would you like the chance of helping a man who's just come out of prison?' she asked.

'I'm very short at the moment, I'm afraid.'

'No, it's not cash he wants. It's a home.'

'A home?' said Henry. 'What has that got to do with me?'

'He's quite willing to pay for his board and lodging but he wants to be taken back into society and, as you're a widower with a housekeeper, we wondered if you'd care to help him.'

'You say he's just come out of prison. What for?'

'We don't know exactly. Of course we can find all the details from the police. He says it's for fraud of one kind or another.'

'D'you mean he's been in more than once?'

'He says so.'

'I can't have a criminal about the house. For one thing it wouldn't be fair to my next door neighbours. You, for instance.'

'How are these people to get back into society if people like us don't help them?'

'Forgive me saying so,' said Henry, 'if you're so keen on helping him, why don't you have him yourself? You've got a spare room.'

'We also have two young daughters,' said Douglas. 'He'd pay quite well, by the way.'

'My housekeeper would leave first thing in the morning.'

'Need you tell her his antecedents until she's got to know him?'

'Suppose he walked off with her savings and I hadn't told her anything about him. I'd have to make it good to her, wouldn't I?'

'Mrs Mountjoy is a nice friendly woman.'

'Of course she is,' said Henry, 'or I wouldn't have her.'

'But if you explained to her how important it was to help

ex-prisoners, don't you think she might have compassion enough to agree?'

'I'm not sure that *I* agree. It's all very well to talk about having ex-prisoners. What about helping the people they've burgled or assaulted or cheated? Nobody talks much about that. You don't go to prison these days unless you've asked for it. And if they want to find their own way back into society when they come out of gaol, they've got to make their own plans for doing so. As a matter of fact, I don't see why we *should* have them back in society. I don't want them back. I say, this sherry needs something to go with it more than your other. You couldn't do me a bit of hot buttered toast, I suppose?'

'If you're as hungry as all that,' said Douglas, 'why didn't you ask your Mrs Mountjoy to make you a piece of buttered toast before you came here?'

'It's her evening off. That's why I thought it so good of you to invite me to stay and have dinner with you. A little soup and bread and cheese will do me nicely. Oh, and if you've got an apple.'

'Apples are quite tasteless at the moment,' said Sheila, 'and not worth buying at 15 or 18 or 20p a pound.'

'D'you mean to say you haven't got an apple or a bar of chocolate in the house?'

'No, we haven't.'

'But you must have a bit of bread.'

'We might have a whole loaf,' said Sheila.

'And some butter, I suppose. Or have you been reduced to margarine?'

'That will be the next step,' said Douglas.

'As a matter of fact,' said Sheila, 'we do use margarine for cooking.'

'I don't care for the stuff,' said Henry. 'Perhaps it's all right in cooking but I prefer my hot buttered toast with real butter.'

'Well,' said Sheila, 'if you promise to go as soon as you've eaten it, I'll go and make you a piece.'

'I say that's a bit hard, "Promise to go." I hope I'm not outstaying my welcome.'

'Not in the least, but I know Theo will be hungry and I shall want to give him his dinner.'

'Well, of course. I'll be off in a flash as soon as I've had it.'

Sheila started to leave the room.

'I suppose you haven't got any of that rather nice stuff? What's it called? Gentlemen's Relish.'

'We haven't used that for a long time.'

'Have you had any chicken lately? I know that you're awfully good at making liver paté. You haven't a bit of that left, I suppose?'

'We have, as a matter of fact,' said Sheila, 'but I'm afraid it's reserved for Theo. He loves it.'

'I don't want a lot,' said Henry. 'Just show it the toast.'

Sheila left the room for the kitchen.

'You must think I'm an awful scrounger,' said Henry when she'd left. 'It's all very well for chaps like you with a loving wife and daughters only too anxious to supply your slightest wish, but I have to pay someone to look after me.'

'Mrs Mountjoy does you quite well, doesn't she?'

'Oh, she's all right,' said Henry, 'but I have to take what she gives me and say thank you and, if she's not feeling in the mood, she doesn't bother very much. I don't need a lot but I do like nice food.'

'If she isn't a good enough cook why don't you change her?'

'She's cheap. I couldn't get anyone else at her price. Unless of course I had somebody who'd just left prison.'

'That's an idea,' said Douglas, 'then my fellow might marry her and they could both look after you.'

'They'd probably tie me up and dump me in the water butt and run off with my stamp collection.'

'I'd forgotten about that,' said Douglas. 'If you're so hard up, why don't you sell it? Stamps are worth quite a lot, I believe. If you've got the right ones.'

'I've got the right ones,' said Henry. 'Who said I was hard up?'

'You give every appearance of being hard up,' said Douglas.

'Because I come scrounging off you?' said Henry. 'Don't you believe it. Scrounging has nothing to do with being hard up. I don't mind admitting that I'm a born scrounger. I like touching people. I like getting something for nothing. You've got no idea what a kick it gave me when Sheila went off to make me some toast. I am hungry and I shall enjoy it very much. Even better if she puts a bit of that paté on it. But I get just as much of a kick out of the knowledge that I'm scrounging as I do from the actual thing I've scrounged. I don't know why I'm telling you this. It can't be the sherry. By the way, don't you think it was rather neat the way I tried to invite myself to dinner?'

'I could call it many things,' said Douglas, 'but neat is not one of them. But it's nice to be able to talk to you frankly. One thing I can tell you which I'm sure will please you. D'you know how Sheila and I refer to you?'

'Scrounging Henry, I expect.'

'You're absolutely right. I wonder if anybody's put his hobbies in *Who's Who* as scrounging. I've never seen it yet.'

At that moment Sheila came back with a piece of hot buttered toast.

'Thank you, my dear,' said Henry. 'It is good of you. I hope it wasn't too much trouble.'

'He hopes nothing of the sort,' said Douglas. 'He's just admitted to me that he's a born scrounger and enjoys the process. He actually gloated over the fact that you went into the kitchen simply to make him a piece of hot buttered toast.'

'Then,' said Sheila, 'I'm glad I didn't put any paté on it. I very nearly yielded.'

'What a shame,' said Henry. 'Never mind. D'you think I could have a bit more of that sherry. I must say it's pretty

36

awful muck but there's nothing else, is there? Nothing you're prepared to produce, that is.'

'As a matter of fact,' said Douglas, 'I have one bottle of Chateau Lafite 1953.'

'Oh you mustn't open that for me,' said Henry.

'Have no fear. We are keeping that till we have something really to celebrate.'

'As far as I can see,' said Henry, 'all you'll be able to celebrate today will be my leaving you. That would hardly merit a bottle of Chateau Lafite 1953. I say, this toast is good. I am glad I asked for it. Have you a toaster or do you do it under the grill?'

'As a matter of fact we're on our last toaster.'

'Your last? How d'you mean?'

'We were given about seventeen as wedding presents. We gave some of them away. We're beginning to regret that now. We thought they'd last the whole of our lives.'

'There's just one thing. I meant to ask you to cut the crusts off. Don't worry. I can manage. If you'd just let me have a finger napkin to wipe my hands. They've got a little greasy with the butter. And it's good of you to have used butter and not margarine.'

'If Sheila could have heard what you've just told me she wouldn't have used anything. Only a little stale fat.'

'Oh she's much too kind for that, however much I deserve it. I hope my confession isn't going to alter our relationship.'

'It will make it much easier,' said Douglas. 'It will be so much easier to say No.'

'But neither of you are made like that. You aren't the sort of people to say No. And when you talk it over you'll be rather sorry for me. After all, you'll say, it can't be much of a life having to scrounge all the time. The poor fellow did lose his wife. At any rate I don't do anything illegal like the fellow you tried to foist on me.'

Henry finished his toast and his glass of sherry, wiped his mouth with his handkerchief and got up.

'Well, I suppose, if there's nothing else I can do you for tonight, I'd better start making tracks. So very nice to have seen you both. More than sorry that I can't stop to dinner. It was good of you to have asked me.'

Douglas showed him to the front door and he left. 'I wonder why he said all that,' he said when he was back with Sheila. 'He must have been here two years. Why choose today?'

'I should have thought that two years was just about the right time,' said Sheila. 'He obviously enjoys doing it but there's no point in doing it until his reputation as a scrounger is firmly accepted.'

'That didn't take him two years,' said Douglas.

Then Theo came back into the room. 'You don't know of a retired mechanic in the neighbourhood, do you by any chance, who would like to earn a bit of money in his spare time? I can't pay much at the moment but I desperately need some help.'

'I do as a matter of fact,' said Douglas. 'But I think he'd be too dangerous for you to employ.'

'Dangerous!' said Theo. 'What on earth d'you mean?'

'He's an ex-criminal. He may still be a criminal for aught I know. Just come out of gaol. At least so he says.'

'Well, I can look after myself,' said Theo.

'Can you now? You're an inventor. An inventor has secrets of one kind or another. What's there to prevent this chap stealing them? I'm sure he's perfectly capable of it.'

'I see,' said Theo. 'You have got a point there. But if I kept the invention side of my business quite separate and didn't let him have anything to do with it, wouldn't that be safe?'

'How separate?' asked Douglas. 'You could lock all the things up of course, but I would have thought that this chap would have been perfectly capable of breaking in or having a key made for the lock or whatever.'

'D'you think he's a good mechanic?'

'I haven't the faintest idea. I don't really know if he's a mechanic at all. It was just what he told me.'

'Tell me exactly what happened.'

So Douglas told Theo the story of Edward.

'How much d'you think he'd want?' asked Theo.

'He wouldn't want very much at the moment. That's why I thought of him. What he said he wants is to get back into society. He *says* that he's going to go straight from now on, but I've no doubt that's what they all say and I think this chap's quite as unscrupulous as our Henry next door.'

'Henry doesn't steal surely?'

'Oh good gracious no. I meant that your prospective employee was as unscrupulous over his stealing as Henry is over his scrounging. On the whole I wouldn't recommend him.'

'D'you think I could see him?' asked Theo. 'I could tell in ten minutes whether he was the sort of chap I wanted as far as the work was concerned.'

'I couldn't tell in an hour whether he's going to lead an honest life in the future. My guess is that he isn't. Or at any rate that, even if he really intends to – as to which I have no idea – if temptation came his way, he'd be likely to fall for it. Not the sort of man I'd care to have access to my secrets.'

'How much d'you think he'd want?'

'That depends,' said Douglas. 'I think he'd take a very low wage at first if we let him into the house. Had him to meals occasionally and that sort of thing. I think he'd do it to get in with us.'

'D'you mean he'd take ten or fifteen pounds a week?'

'I think he probably would. You see he's got plenty of money at the moment. That's one thing I do know because I've seen it. He brought it out and showed it to me.'

'How much?'

'£750 about.'

'Good God! He must be an extraordinary chap.'

'I should say that he was. Of course he's the first criminal whom I've met to my knowledge. It may be that they're all like that. And then, you see, I don't even know that he is a criminal. He must be a liar because either he's lying to me when he said he came from prison or he lied in order to commit his crime.'

'A burglar doesn't have to lie,' said Theo, 'except when he's caught and tries to put up an alibi.'

'I don't *think* this chap's a burglar. I think he's what they call a con man. He says he's cheated a lot of banks. He told me how he did it. I've a feeling that what he said was true, but it wouldn't surprise me in the least to find that it wasn't and that he was some kind of a writer or journalist out to get copy. You know the sort of thing I mean. Talking like he did to me to various people and then writing an article to show the effect it had on them. I never thought of it but he may be doing a sort of "candid camera" lark.'

'He sounds an amusing person to meet,' said Theo. 'D'you think there'd be any objection to my going to see him?'

'I don't know where he is.'

'You said he'd be staying at the best country house hotel in the neighbourhood. That means he must be at Holly Towers. What's his name?'

'He's got so many,' said Douglas. 'Let me see. What was the first name he gave me? Oh, I remember. It was Edward Livermore. By the time we'd reached Redhill I was thinking of him as Wilberforce. So what he's registered under I haven't the faintest idea.'

'D'you mind if I ring him?' asked Theo.

'What d'you think?' asked Douglas, looking at Sheila.

'I suppose it can't do much harm,' she said. 'And, after all, we are asked to give them jobs. I've been preaching that for years and, now we're faced with it, I realise that it's other people I want to give them jobs. However, if Theo doesn't mind the risk and you don't, I'll agree.'

Theo picked up the receiver and dialled the number of Holly Towers. 'Have you a Mr Livermore just come to stay with you?' he asked.

'Yes,' said the receptionist. 'He came in about an hour ago.'

'Could I speak to him, please?'

'Certainly. Who shall I say wants him?'

Theo gave his name. A moment later :

'Hullo,' said Edward. 'It's very good of you to ring me up, Mr Barton. I didn't think you would. You must be my fellow passenger. It can't be anybody else because nobody knows I'm staying here.'

'As a matter of fact,' said Theo, 'it's Theodore Barton speaking. My father told me that you were a mechanic and that you might be wanting a job.'

'How kind of him. Yes, that's indeed the case. Have you got a garage?'

'No. A workshop.' Theo put his hand over the mouthpiece and said quietly : 'Shall I go over to him or can I ask him here?'

'Go over to him, of course.'

'I was thinking of the petrol. It's at least five miles. I shall have to use the car and from what you tell me he can easily afford a taxi.'

'Are you still there?'

'Yes,' said Theo, 'I was just trying to think of the best way of our meeting.'

'That's as you like,' said Edward. 'I'll come over to you or you can come over here. Come and have dinner with me to-night, if you like. It's still on.'

'He's asked me to dinner,' said Theo. 'D'you think the petrol will about equal the value of the dinner I don't eat? That's if you can save it.'

'Ale, Squeery?' said Sheila.

Douglas hesitated for a moment and then nodded.

When Nicholas Nickleby went to stay with Mr and Mrs Squeers at Dotheboys Hall and was having dinner with them on the night of his arrival, Dickens enthusiasts will remember that Mrs Squeers looked at her husband and said, "Ale, Squeery?". She meant, not did he, Squeers, want any ale, but was she to give any to Nicholas. The reply was, 'Yes, one glass' and that is what Nicholas got. Douglas and Sheila, who were both keen Dickensians, found it an extremely useful way of asking each other questions about the children in their presence, when they were young, without their knowing what was meant by the question. For example, when one of the twins wanted some more pudding and Douglas who was serving it was not sure whether she had had enough, he would look at Sheila and say, 'Ale, Squeery?' and, if she nodded, the child would get the pudding. And vice versa. Although Theo knew all about the device, they still occasionally used it for fun. It is a method of communication which is very useful between husbands and wives or people who know each other well. It can be applied on all sorts of occasions wholly unconnected with children. If you are given an invitation or are not sure whether to extend an invitation and want to consult your spouse on the subject, all you've got to do is to say, 'Ale Squeery?'. If the answer is Yes, you accept or extend the invitation and, if the answer is No, you don't. Usually it has to be done as an aside.

On this occasion Theo saw his father nod and so he accepted the invitation.

CHAPTER THREE

Taken On

Holly Towers was a typically pretentious country house hotel. But its standard varied and it found its way in and out of the Good Food Guide with regularity. At the moment when Theo went to dine with Edward it would not have been in the Guide if the proprietors of that publication had known that there was going to be a change of management. The new management had plenty of money but a very poor idea of how to run a hotel successfully. As with battalions and businesses the standard of service comes from the top, so, if the manager doesn't know how to treat his guests nor do the waiters or the chambermaids. A good example of the standard of service came when the coffee was being served. Edward said that he would like his black with a little cream.

'This is milk,' said the waiter.

'I thought it was,' said Edward. 'I'd prefer a little cream.'

'We don't serve cream with black coffee,' said the waiter.

'Will you be good enough to ask the head waiter to come and speak to me,' said Edward. The waiter said nothing but left the table. He came back a few minutes later and said : 'The head waiter says : "Let them have it".'

Theo was quite interested in food but on this occasion he didn't mind in the least what sort of dinner it was. He only wanted to know what sort of man he was meeting. In particular, was he a good mechanic? Did he really understand what mechanical and electrical engineering were all about? Theo found that he did. That was the first hurdle. Edward would be able to do what Theo wanted. The second hurdle was rather more difficult. But Edward was prepared to help.

'Now I expect you'd like to talk about terms,' he said.

'Yes,' said Theo and waited.

'Has your father told you all about me?'

'He's told me what you told him,' said Theo, 'as far as he could remember.'

'You mean,' said Edward, 'your father conveyed to you that he was not sure if what I told him was true.'

'Well, he's only met you once and that on a railway journey for an hour or so.'

'Don't apologise, please. It's very natural that he should want to know whether I was telling the truth or not. Particularly as I said I had been to gaol several times.'

'Have you?' asked Theo.

'I have indeed.'

'D'you mind my asking some questions about it?'

'I should welcome them.'

'What made you go in the first place?'

'I must think,' said Edward. 'You see, the difficulty is that I've told so many stories about that, that at this stage it is difficult to remember which is the true one. I take it you would prefer the true one.'

'If you can manage it,' said Theo.

'Well, I can't be absolutely sure,' said Edward, 'but I think it was like this. I had been what they call well-educated and was about your age. Up till then I had always done what my parents suggested and, as they suggested that I should try to make banking my career, into a bank I went. No, I wasn't tempted in the first instance by the thousands of pounds lying around me, but I did find that my progress was not fast enough and that the early work they put me on was not interesting

44

enough. Once or twice I had been allowed to act as cashier while a lot of the regular cashiers were sick and it was from one particular customer that I learned the way of getting rich quick. He didn't know it of course, but he introduced me to kite-flying. He did my unfortunate manager down for between fifty and sixty thousand pounds. Some of the cheques I cashed for him myself and naturally before giving him the money I asked the manager for permission. I always got it. I subsequently learned that, after he was in debt to the extent of about forty thousand pounds, the manager realised what was happening. He was too frightened to let the head office know and must have prayed every night – as no doubt did the customer – that the horses would run faster or the gambles come off better than they had done in the past. But they didn't. And when the debt was nearly sixty thousand pounds, the manager had to make a clean breast of it to head office. It seemed such a simple way of making money that I couldn't resist trying it myself. I was no longer living at home and I simply gave in my notice and sent a note to my parents that I thought I was going into business on my own account and that I'd let them know in due course how I was getting on. I got on very well. Some of my horses actually came in at quite good odds. The result was that my first attempt at kite-flying was wholly successful. The bank lost nothing and I made several thousand pounds. I gave my parents a beautiful silver dish as a silver wedding present. But gamblers are quite right when they say it is dangerous to win the first time. You think your luck will hold but it never does. As a result of my first effort I became quite a good customer at one of the banks and they were quite prepared to let me have quite a lot of credit. In the end I did them down for a hundred thousand pounds and was only able to keep about a thousand myself, and, although as far as was known it was a first offence, I got three years for it at the age of twenty-five. I'm not boring you?'

'Not in the least,' said Theo.

'I don't suppose you've ever spoken to a con man before?'

'Not to my knowledge.'

'And you find it a bit of a thrill, I expect?'

'Yes, I do.'

'Well, I strongly advise you not to become one. You've no idea what it's like going to prison for the first time. It's a terrible experience for most people. Certainly it is for anybody who's had a decent home before going there. The Home Office says that one of the first aims of those responsible for keeping people in prison is "to ensure that the inmate's sense of dignity is not assailed beyond that which is inevitable in the curtailment of freedom." I learned that bit by heart. Let me tell you how it compares with what really happens to a man who is sentenced to imprisonment. He is taken from the dock to a cell below where he will be locked up. He has already been searched but he will be searched again to be sure that he's not got any means of committing suicide. He will then be handcuffed to another prisoner and taken to the local prison. This may be several hours after he has been sentenced. Only if he is very lucky will he get a meal or even a cup of tea before he reaches the prison. On arrival at the prison he will be lined up with many others to await the Reception procedure. He may be locked in a small room or box about four foot square to await this procedure. He will then be required to take a bath and to hand over his clothes and private possessions and to dress in prison clothing which will probably be shabby, secondhand and ill-fitting. At this point he will be given a meal and taken to his cell. Probably he will be locked in a cell with one or two others who may well have physical habits which he finds unacceptable and whose mental processes may differ greatly from what he is used to. The next morning he will be woken up at about six-thirty a.m. by a bell ringing on the landing. He will be expected to get up at once, wash in cold water, dress and make his bed. In due course he will take part in slopping out.

46

For this purpose the cell will be unlocked and with all the other prisoners he will carry out his chamber pot, in which he will have done everything that may have been necessary, he will take it along the landing and pour it into the sluice, rinse out the pot and return to his cell. Since the diet is largely farinaceous the smell arising from slopping out is enough to put any normal person off his breakfast, however hungry he may have been. Well, I think that should be enough to discourage you.'

'How ghastly,' said Theo when he had finished.

'Don't you think it would be a good idea,' said Edward, 'if when the Government sent round their literature about the Common Market they had also sent a description of a first day in prison to every household in the country? It might be interesting to get a similar version from each of the members of the European Economic Community.'

'What about the people who can't read?' said Theo. 'Quite a lot of them go to prison.'

'You're quite right. Television and radio would have to do it for them. But you'd have to do it on all the stations or they'd simply turn to another.'

'They'd probably turn it off, wouldn't they?' said Theo.

'Some would, but the message might get home to a few.'

'You've told me how you started,' said Theo, 'but why did you go back for more?'

'Well, once you get over the shock of it and what it means, it isn't so awful to contemplate going back again. That is, it isn't so awful for some people. I'm inclined to take things as they come. That doesn't mean to say I wasn't affected by my first forty-eight hours inside. I was. But once you know the worst, you know whether you can take it. I found that I could. I didn't want to take a steady job. I wasn't in the least bitter about being sent to prison. After all, I had asked for it. I knew I was breaking the rules, but I didn't at the time want to work so hard for a living.'

47

'How many times have you been inside altogether?'

'Five.'

'Then why have you decided to stop?'

'I told your father that it was the smell. That isn't quite true but there's something in it. I can't pretend that I've reformed and that I want to fulfil my social obligations. I don't think anyone can reform. You can't change your mentality. No, I think it's just this. I'm over forty and I enjoy life. That is to say, I enjoy life outside prison and I came to the conclusion in the end that I should be happier not going back to prison. That's all it is. The smell was part of it but of course only a small part. I believe it's the same with every man who says he's going to go straight. If I go straight, I shall be no better than I was when I was going crooked. Except to the extent that it will be better for the community if I do go straight. I shall be a more useful member of it. In that sense I'll be better. But I shan't be better in the moral sense in any way. I shall simply be behaving in accordance with the rules for my own benefit.'

'If it's not impertinent for a very young man like me,' said Theo, 'to talk to you like this, why are you being so frank with me?'

'That's quite simple. Because I want something out of you. I think you're an intelligent young man and I want to impress you with the fact that I'm not going to take up crime again. Now it isn't easy for a man with five previous convictions to get into society again and I must admit that I was very struck with your father when I met him in the train and I said to myself that, if I could get into his family, it would be a marvellous opportunity. I don't blame him for not liking the idea at all and I don't suppose your mother liked it any better. Probably worse. But if I've made a good impression on you and you'll take me on to do a job of work in your business it will suit me fine.'

'I can't pay very much,' said Theo.

48

'That doesn't matter. I'd almost pay you to take me on. From my point of view it's getting started in the right place that's so important. I told your father that I wanted to get married. That's absolutely true. There's nothing like marriage to keep a chap on the rails. I may want some help sometimes. Fortunately, I gather, you haven't got a sister of the right age. It might have been awkward if you had. I can't see your parents letting me go on working for you if you had. That, of course, is one of my serious problems. What respectable girl would want to marry a man with five previous convictions? With no guarantee except his word that there won't be any more in the future. And what's my word worth to anybody who doesn't know me? I shall ask you the same question as I asked your father. If I come across a woman I like, am I to tell her straightaway what my history is? In which case she will probably have nothing more to do with me. Or am I to wait until there is some affection between us? What would you advise?'

'I haven't the faintest idea,' said Theo. 'I only thank God that it will never happen to me. After your description of your first day in prison I shall never take a chance of going there.'

'I doubt if there will ever be any question of your going to prison,' said Edward. 'But you can never be certain what will happen to you in life.'

'Except when you drive a car,' said Theo, 'you can always make certain that you stand no risk of going to prison.'

'Can you? Suppose you married a girl who turned out to be a shoplifter. She may not have been one when you married her but later on the temptation becomes too great. She gets several convictions and there's a danger that on the next one she will be sent to prison. Wouldn't you try and protect her? In which case you might find yourself charged with telling lies to prevent her arrest or something of that sort. Suppose she had stolen a mink coat and you'd got it in your house and you were trying to get it back to the true owner surreptitiously but in the meantime the police come to your house. Your wife has three previous convictions and now she's stolen the mink coat. Aren't you going to deny that the coat's on the premises? Aren't you going to confirm your wife's story that she was with you at the time it was said that she stole it? I'm sure that's what you'd want to do and I hope that's what you would do. If you were found out, you might very well go to prison yourself. But you'd help your wife, wouldn't you, in spite of the impression which I have made on you of my story of the first twenty-four hours in prison?'

'You're quite right. It's not as easy as I thought. Getting down to business, I can only offer you to begin with what you'd probably call pocket money. Ten to fifteen pounds a week. My business won't stand any more.'

'That will be fine. When can I start?'

CHAPTER FOUR

_____

A Problem for Henry

While Theo was on his way to interview Edward, Henry had made his way sadly back to his house. There he found Mrs Mountjoy enjoying a supper of fried eggs, bacon, sausage, tomato, liver, with a piece of fried bread. The smell was most inviting. Henry came into the room where she was enjoying her meal, waited for half a minute and then said rather tentatively : 'I suppose,—' Mrs Mountjoy did not look up, but she spoke after finishing her mouthful.

'Shut your gob,' she said, not in the way those words are usually said but in a most precise and genteel manner, reminiscent of 'papa, potatoes, prunes and prisms'.

'Mrs M,' Henry began to protest, but she interrupted, having first put down her knife and fork meaningfully. Then she turned round to face him.

'How often have I told you,' she said, 'what my husband, the late Mr M, warned me in Darkest Africa. Never get between an animal and its food. Now that applies as much to human beings as it does to grisly bears, so b – buzz off.'

Henry did as he was told and went to his study. There he found a half-full box of Black Magic chocolates. He hesitated for a moment and then took one. It was fatal. By the time Mrs Mountjoy had finished her supper he was not really hungry at all. He was in his study when she came to him.

'It was no go,' he said. 'I told them it was your evening off but they just wouldn't play.'

'I've done you a welsh rarebit,' she said. 'You'd better have it before it gets cold. And the coffee's still hot.'

A quarter of an hour previously Henry would have been overjoyed at the information and fallen upon the food ravenously.

'It's very good of you, Mrs M,' he said.

'It's what you pay me for, Mr Bunting, and, as my late husband Mr M used to say, the labourer is worthy of his hire.'

'You're worth a good deal more to me, Mrs M, than what I pay you.'

'I'm well aware of that,' she said, 'but you pay me in kind. What I don't get in cash I get in power. If you paid me a decent wage I'd have to do what you told me or get out. As it is, you have to do what I tell you, and Mr M, my late husband, you know, being dead I have to turn to someone and you suit me very well. I can't say that you look like Mr M. You don't. He was a tall and good-looking man and even his oldest clothes fitted him to perfection. He always looked smart even when he was gardening.

'I'm afraid no one could say that of me,' said Henry.

'No one is saying it of you,' said Mrs Mountjoy. 'But you have one thing in common. Although you haven't a moustache, you make much the same noise eating your soup as he did. I never could abide it but it has a fatal fascination for me and I listen for it. Once or twice when you've been having your food alone I've put my head round the door just to hear it. Now your welsh rarebit will be a soggy mess. Ah, you've been at the chocolates, I see. How many more times have I got to tell you not to eat them before dinner?'

'I'm sorry, Mrs M,' said Henry, 'but I did come to you first.'

'Don't remind me. It nearly spoiled my supper but fortunately not quite. And that bacon was as crisp as I've ever tasted. And the fried bread – oh boy. Now run along. Would you like a little stewed apple after it?'

'I don't think so, thanks. I'm not really very peckish.'

'I'll come and watch you eat it to see that you don't waste any.'

They went together to the kitchen where they usually had their meals when they had no visitors.

'The Bartons are in a bad way, I think,' he said, after he'd started his welsh rarebit. 'They've started on British sherry. Oh, good Lord, I quite forgot. They said I could take the remainder of the bottle back with me. I'll go back for it when I've finished this.'

'British sherry? We wouldn't have it in the house.'

'I didn't want it for ourselves,' said Henry, 'but we've got some empty Manzanilla bottles and I thought I would pour it into one of those and give it to friends.'

'An Amontillado bottle would be better. It's more sickly.'

'Once again you're right, Mrs M,' said Henry. 'Your husband taught you a lot, I see.'

'Fiddlesticks, it was I who taught him. He knew nothing whatever about wine when I married him. He didn't know much when he died. He wasn't a good learner. But he could tell a claret from a burgundy provided he saw the shape of the bottle.'

'That's not a bad idea,' said Henry. 'Douglas rather fancies himself as an expert. Next time they come to dinner let's pour some burgundy into a claret bottle. I'll bet he falls for it.'

'You're not thinking of having them for dinner, after the way they've treated you tonight?'

'Well, he might be rather awkward about that planning permission we want over the field. I think perhaps we'll try to soften them up when the times comes. D'you know, it wouldn't surprise me if they started taking in paying guests. They really are feeling the draught. As a matter of fact, they tried to foist one on me. You wouldn't believe it. He actually asked me if we'd take in a gaolbird. I said you wouldn't hear of it.'

'When did I give you permission to say that?'

'I felt sure you wouldn't.'

'As a matter of fact it would be most interesting. I've never seen a gaolbird at close quarters, except on the telly. When you go round to fetch the sherry, you tell them I'd be prepared to consider it. So long as it's not a murderer or anybody like that.'

'But he might steal.'

'You're insured, aren't you?'

'Yes, but wouldn't you hate the idea, when you couldn't find something, of not knowing whether it had been stolen or not? It's bad enough when the window-cleaners have been and you can't find a silver ash tray or something. But with someone actually living in the house, you'd be like that the whole time. One is always missing something.'

'When did we last miss anything?'

'You know what I mean.'

'I do not know what you mean. You seem to be suggesting that I'm careless and put things in the wrong place. If anyone in this house puts things in the wrong place it's not me.'

'It would mean a lot of extra work for you.'

'I'd get paid for it. Now, if you've finished, run along next door and tell them we're interested in the proposition.'

'D'you really mean it?'

'Of course I do. The late Mr M used to say: "Do noble deeds, not dream them all day long".'

'Very well, if you say so,' said Henry. And a few minutes later he was on his way to the Bartons. He was met at the door by Douglas who held a half empty bottle of sherry in his hand.

'You've come for this, I suppose?' he said, and held it out.

'How kind,' said Henry, 'but there was another thing as well. Could I come in for a minute?'

'Very well,' said Douglas resignedly, and they went into the sitting room.

'Mrs Mountjoy says,' began Henry, when Sheila interrupted him.

'I thought this was her night out,' she said.

'Her night *off*,' said Henry. 'She preferred to have it at home.'

'So you had to make your own supper.'

'As a matter of fact I didn't. She rustled me up something. But, when I told her about your ex-criminal, she said she'd be prepared to consider having him as a paying guest.'

'Good gracious.'

'I think she's intrigued,' said Henry. 'She watches all the crime plays and Z Cars and all that and she's dying to see what a criminal is like at close quarters. When I warned her of the possible consequences, she brushed my objections aside.'

'What about you? D'you like the idea?' Sheila said.

'I can't say that I do, but if I want to keep Mrs Mountjoy I have to like her ideas.'

'As a matter of fact, Theo's dining with him at the moment at Holly Towers. He wants to give him a job. If he does, it would be quite convenient for him if he lives next door.'

'That would be something,' said Henry. 'We'd all be in it together.'

They hadn't been discussing the matter very much longer when Theo returned.

'Well?' said Douglas. 'What did you make of him? You can speak quite freely. Henry knows all about it.'

'As a matter of fact,' said Theo, 'I liked him very much. I think he's a very decent chap. And I would say that he's absolutely honest.'

'What on earth d'you mean? He's got at least five previous convictions for crime and I don't suppose he was caught every time.'

'I mean in what he says. He told me roughly how he came to start and why he's determined to stop. And he didn't try any of that nonsense about having reformed and all that stuff.'

'It isn't stuff,' said Sheila. 'Quite a number of ex-prisoners do reform.'

'Depends what you mean by reform,' said Theo. 'What he says is that you can't reform in the sense that your morals can't change, but you can decide for reasons of your own not to commit any more crimes. And I believe him. At any rate I've offered him a job and he's going to start tomorrow.'

'That's interesting,' said Douglas. 'Henry's just come round to say that he's prepared to take him as a paying guest.'

'That will be splendid,' said Theo. 'He'll be able to start early in the morning.'

'That isn't brandy by any chance that you're drinking?' asked Henry.

'It was,' said Douglas, 'but I'm afraid we've just finished the dregs of the bottle.'

'Never mind,' said Henry. 'You haven't a spot of whisky, I suppose?'

'We have,' said Sheila, 'but I'm afraid we've got to keep it for some people who are coming to dinner on Saturday.'

'You sure they drink whisky?'

'Quite.'

'Who are they, by the way?'

'The Ringways.'

'Funny thing,' said Henry, 'I'd heard they've gone on the wagon.'

'They didn't mention it when they accepted our invitation.'

'Well, they wouldn't, would they? Perhaps I could ring them up and ask them.'

'Not from here,' said Douglas.

'I feel a bit down at the moment,' said Henry. 'I could do with a pick-me-up. No gin, I suppose?'

Douglas looked at Sheila. 'Ale, Squeery?' he said. She nodded. 'Well, Henry,' said Douglas, 'as you know, we've been trying to economise and the other day I got a bottle of gin of some unknown make and we've still got most of it left. You can have some of that if you like.'

'I say, that's uncommonly good of you.'

'You may not think so when you've drunk it. It tasted to us like methylated spirits.'

'It can't be as bad as that.'

'Theo, would you like to fetch the bottle and a clean glass?' said Sheila.

Theo went out and soon came back with them.

'What would you like with it? I should advise tonic or ginger ale. That takes away the taste to some extent.'

'No, I think I'll have it neat,' said Henry. 'When I've missed my dinner, I want something to buck me up.'

'At your own risk,' said Douglas, and he poured him out a generous glass.

'Your very good health,' said Henry, and he took a cautious sip. 'Good God,' he said. 'It *is* methylated spirits.'

'The wine merchant did tell me it was an acquired taste.'

'It's not one I'm going to acquire, thank you very much. Will you forgive me if I don't finish it?'

'Pity,' said Douglas. 'We were going to offer you the rest of the bottle.'

'No, thank you very much.'

'Why don't you take it,' said Theo, 'and put it into an empty bottle of a well-known brand?'

'You mean to offer to my friends? Would your parents do a thing like that?'

'No,' said Douglas, 'I don't think we would.'

'Then why should you think that I'd do such a thing?'

'Well,' said Theo, 'if you do it with claret and burgundy I don't see why you shouldn't with gin.'

'What did you say?' said Henry.

Theo repeated it.

'What on earth makes you say that?'

'Wouldn't you?' said Theo. 'That's what you said to Mrs

Mountjoy, isn't it? About a quarter of an hour ago. I was listening to you as I came along in the car.'

'What on earth d'you mean?' said Henry.

'I've made one of those snooping devices. It'll pick up sound within about a quarter of a mile.'

'But you must have fitted a microphone into our house then?'

'No,' said Theo, 'that's the old-fashioned way. You see, when you talk or make any noise sound waves start to reverberate, although they peter out after a distance. But that depends on how loud they are and what is surrounding them – I mean if you'd like to line all your walls with half inch lead it would be pretty safe.'

'But this is monstrous,' said Henry. 'How much of my conversation have you been listening to?'

'As a matter of fact,' said Theo, 'I haven't perfected it yet and it was just a bit of luck that I heard you. I wasn't quite sure that it was you, but I thought it was and I'm glad I was right.'

'They'll have to ban an invention like this,' said Henry.

'That's why I want to perfect it and sell it before they do.'

'What else have you heard us say?'

'Nothing really, as a matter of fact. I was just playing with it as I was on my way home when I suddenly heard you. At least I felt sure it was your voice. By the way, Dad, d'you think you'll be able to tell when he tries it on?'

'I very much doubt it,' said Douglas. 'It depends of course on what the claret or burgundy is. I mean, I don't suppose I'd mistake a superb burgundy for a claret or vice versa but with some nondescript wine I think many of the experts could go wrong and would only have a fifty-fifty chance of being right.'

'But this is awful,' said Henry. 'I'll never be able to say anything at home in case you're listening.'

'I wasn't doing it deliberately,' said Theo. 'It just happened. Of course I won't do it deliberately in the future.'

'How am I to be sure?'

'You've got to take his word for it,' said Douglas.

'I think I'll be going back,' said Henry. 'I'll have to break the news to Mrs M. She'll probably leave.'

'Shall I get Edward to come and see you in the morning?' said Theo.

'Edward?'

'Yes, the criminal chap.'

'The evening would be better,' said Henry.

'Very well.'

Henry started to go and then remembered the bottle of sherry. As he took it he said to Theo: 'You didn't hear what I said about this, I suppose?'

'No,' said Theo, 'I didn't.'

'Good,' said Henry. 'Goodbye all.' And he left.

After he'd gone Douglas asked Theo how long he'd perfected his new invention.

'I haven't perfected it,' said Theo. 'As a matter of fact, it was only a chance in a thousand that it came off this evening. That's why I haven't said anything to you about it yet. But I'm obviously very close to it.'

'Poor old Henry. I hope he doesn't lose Mrs Mountjoy. She'd be very difficult to replace.'

But Henry had made up his mind about one thing. He was not going to tell Mrs Mountjoy anything about it, unless he was absolutely forced to do so.

CHAPTER FIVE

Economic Pressures

'I suppose,' said Sheila the next morning to Douglas, 'that we couldn't persuade your Mr Livermore to come and talk to our Group? It would be tremendously helpful to have the criminal's view put before us at first hand. At the moment we only get it from probation officers and books and so on.'

'Then he'd have to disclose to the whole neighbourhood who he was and I don't suppose he'd want to do that,' said Douglas.

'Couldn't he wear a mask or something when he comes to speak to us so that people won't know who he is?'

'Or a beard or a moustache,' said Douglas. 'I suppose he could do that.'

'I wonder if he'd be willing?'

'We could ask,' said Douglas. 'That won't do any harm. But I must say that what is worrying me now has nothing whatever to do with him. It's Theo's invention. He'll have to go very carefully with it. He oughtn't to have told Henry about it. I'll go and see him and persuade him not to tell anybody else. It's very worrying.'

'What are you so frightened of?'

'To tell you the truth,' said Douglas, 'I'm worried sick that he might be kidnapped.'

'Kidnapped? By whom?'

'By a foreign power or by a gang of criminals. He could be

invaluable to either. There's only one way of stopping that.'

'What's that?'

'By making the invention over to the Government as quickly as possible and letting everybody know that the Government has the secret. Once that was made public, Theo would be reasonably safe. It is like the hazard of nuclear power. Everybody will get hold of the secret in time but until the knowledge is fairly widespread, a gang of criminals might think it worth while to kidnap him and make early and immediate use of the knowledge. I don't know if Theo realises the danger he may be in. I must have a word with him at once.'

But before Douglas could go to see Theo, he came to see his parents.

'I'm terribly sorry about that nonsense I talked last night. I ought to have thought that it might have worried you. Did it?'

'What d'you mean, nonsense? D'you mean to say that all that listening-in stuff isn't true?'

'Of course it isn't. It's physically impossible. If you haven't got a microphone, you'd have to make a person's voice radioactive in itself. And I don't know how they're ever going to do that.'

'What about the burgundy and the claret? Obviously he had said that.'

'As a matter of fact, some weeks ago I heard him say something of the sort and it was just a lucky guess.'

'You mean it was a pure coincidence that he had actually said it on the occasion he said he had?'

'Yes.'

'Thank God for that,' said Douglas. 'But I think you might have told us before.'

'I'm so sorry, Dad. Yes, I ought to have realised, but it amused me to pull all your legs for a bit. I suppose, if you gave a chap a radioactive lozenge with a particular call sign, you might be able to pick it up while he was actually sucking it, but it would be impossible to make him suck the lozenge

61

when you wanted him to do so. He might never suck lozenges.'

'What about chewing-gum – unfortunately most people are acquiring that habit. I first noticed it in the Australian test team some years ago. Now it seems to have spread to every kind of sport. I don't know why it doesn't impede their breathing. Quite dangerous at rugger, I should have thought, in case they swallowed it. But they never seem to. Provided the victim recovered, I wish somebody would. To stop them. It's a horrible habit.'

'Not as dirty as smoking,' said Theo. 'Or as dangerous.'

'That's true enough,' said Douglas. 'I expect the tobacco companies are investing their money in it. But tell me frankly, what did you think of the chap?'

'He may have been taking me for a ride,' said Theo, 'but I thought he was a very decent fellow. I'd enjoy having him to work for me.'

'Do look out,' said his father. 'You've only seen him for an hour or two and some of the greatest judges have admitted that, even after days in the witness-box, they don't know whether a particular person is telling the truth. But I'm less worried about it now that you've told me that you were only spoofing about your listening device.'

'There's an awful lot to be done with radio, you know, in spite of the amount they've done so far.'

'Is that what you're working on at the moment? Your device that's going to rival cats' eyes, I mean?'

'It's one of them.'

'If it succeeds, you'll become a millionaire.'

'I wish I were. And then you wouldn't have to worry about the school fees and all that. But I'm afraid it will be a couple of years before I can be of any help. At the present rate of striking, that is.'

'Oh, we're all right. But everyone's feeling it at the moment. Even the miners and the printers will have so much deducted from their pay that some of them will begin to wonder whether it's worth it. And these rates – they really are the limit. D'you know, they've doubled.'

'If I closed down my business and got a job,' said Theo, 'I could probably get a thousand or fifteen hundred for the stock and plant. Would you like me to?'

'I wouldn't hear of it,' said Douglas. 'Sorry I mentioned the subject.'

'How much do you have to pay for the twins? At school, I mean?'

'I'm not sure.'

'Now come on, Dad. You must have a pretty good idea.'

'Those fees have of course gone up too. I suppose they're about twelve hundred and fifty a year.'

'For the two of them, d'you mean?'

'I wish they were. No, each.'

'But that's two thousand five hundred a year. How on earth can you manage that?'

'Well, we've managed two thousand, so I suppose somehow or other we can manage two thousand five hundred.'

'I don't know how you managed two thousand. Have you been selling things?'

'I'm not going to be cross-examined,' said Douglas. 'You're an inventor and an engineer, not a barrister.'

'O.K., Dad. But I am sorry about it and I do wish I could do something.'

'Well, you do. You keep yourself. In fact you more than do that with what you pay your mother. It helps out generally with the housekeeping.'

'I'm sorry it isn't more.'

'What's this about housekeeping?' asked Sheila, as she came in.

'I only told Theo that what he paid you was more than enough to keep him.'

'It certainly is.'

'Now, at what time is your assistant coming this morning?

I wonder if you'd mind my having a word with him before he starts with you?' said Sheila.

'Of course not. He'll be here in a moment. You can get hold of him before I do. There's a lot I've got to show him.'

'I'll only be a few minutes,' said Sheila.

So, when Edward arrived, Douglas introduced him to Sheila and she spoke to him after Douglas had left.

'I believe my husband told you about the Group I'm interested in which is dealing with prisons and prisoners and so forth.'

'Yes, he did.'

'I hope you don't mind my asking you this and I quite understand if the answer is No. Would you be prepared to give a talk to our Group? You see, although some of us have been over prisons and have talked to some Governors and prison officers and probation officers and prison visitors and all the rest of them, none of us has ever spoken more than a few words to an actual prisoner. To be given a talk by somebody who knows all about it and is articulate would be a tremendous help to us. But I shall quite understand if you would rather not.'

'Honestly, I don't know,' said Edward. 'Your husband knows why I jumped at the opportunity of meeting you. If I appear before your Group everyone will know me for what I am or rather I hope I can say for what I've been. I shall be labelled. "There he goes," they'll say.'

'That's true. Some people will take a morbid interest,' said Sheila. 'Would it be possible for you to wear a mask or something of that kind when you came to speak to us?'

'D'you think it would be wise? They might think I was going to produce a revolver the next moment. No, but seriously, I don't think I could do that. It would be too uncomfortable. I never wore a mask when I used to hold up banks.'

'To hold up banks?' said Sheila, who could not hide a horrified tone in her voice.

'Not in the way you read in the paper. No, I cheated them. Your husband will explain. Another thing, I think it would be too hot. It's quite hot work talking. If you wore a mask it would be hotter still. It would have to be a fairly big one, otherwise they'd see too many of my features. And then somebody would want to have a peep when I took it off. Besides, I expect I might meet somebody with you and they'd soon put two and two together. No, I think if I were to come and talk to you I should have to come as the real genuine article, in colour and three-dimensional. As a matter of fact, it would be a good idea if some of us went round the schools and colleges and told them what prison was really like. I told your boy, as a matter of fact, and it certainly discouraged him, but of course your type of person doesn't need any discouraging.'

'Not even shoplifters?' said Sheila.

'They never go to prison the first time unless they're part of a gang. As far as I can make out the ordinary private shoplifter can have at least three goes before a sentence of imprisonment is likely. And that would probably be suspended.'

'Well, if you'll think about it,' said Sheila, 'I shall be grateful, but I shall fully understand in the end if you say you would rather not. And now I think Theo's expecting you. You'll find him down in the garden in the workshop there. If you go through this door you'll see it.'

She showed him to the garden and then went back to Douglas. 'I rather like him on first acquaintance,' said Sheila. 'Hadn't we better have Henry to lunch so that they can meet each other?'

'Have we got enough?'

'I'll make a large potato pie, mostly of potato, and we've still got plenty of spinach in the garden. What's the beer position?'

'I'll cycle over to the pub and get a few bottles. Oh, could you lend me a pound out of the housekeeping? I forgot to go to the bank.'

The money problems of the average middle-class family who live upon a fixed income have worsened over the last two years probably more than at any time in English history. Married couples without children can get by at the moment by cutting down extravagances of one kind and another. But married couples with growing children who have already committed them to a particular type of education are in a grim position. Nevertheless it is a fact that the waiting lists for public schools are as full as ever and one can only assume that many of them pay for this luxury out of capital.

It was not snobbery which made the Bartons determined to keep their children in the same scheme of education that they had started in. But they thought it would be extremely bad for the children suddenly to be taken away from their friends and the particular musical education which obtained at the school where they were at the moment. The time might come when it would be literally impossible for them to pay the fees, but they were determined to prevent this time from arriving if it was humanly possible. They had already cut down on letter writing and telephoning before the steep rises of 1975. And after these rises they telephoned and wrote even less.

'It's quite possible,' said Douglas, 'that these latest increases will be self-defeating. I should think that the manufacturers of Christmas cards and charities will be thinking of Christmas with some apprehension. Unless a special reduction is made I think that there's a good chance of Christmas cards coming to an end.'

It was a very long time since the Bartons had visited one of the more expensive restaurants. Nor, indeed, did they go into any of the less expensive ones unless it was essential, and it seldom was. They ate at home or took sandwiches with them. When they visited the girls at school they took them to tea instead of lunch at the local hotel. Lunch for four at the Red Lion would have cost them ten or twelve pounds at least. There was a time when lunch at the Lion was looked on by them as a normal way of living.

Douglas and Sheila were not exceptional people in this respect and, if the present situation continues, it is difficult to see how the proprietors of small restaurants and hotels are going to make a living. In one respect Douglas had not economised. He still went to the same hairdresser. He had been there for many, many years and would have hated the idea of going anywhere else. For twenty-five years no one had cut his hair except an assistant at that particular shop. But now the price had gone up to two pounds for a shampoo and haircut. At the moment he sought to solve that problem by the simple expedient of having his hair cut once in every two months instead of once every month. Sheila had protested from time to time about the hair on his neck but he had refused to be persuaded by her to go more often to a cheaper hairdresser.

One of their greatest problems was Sheila's clothes. Douglas had several well-made suits and could manage very well without getting another. But a woman does need new clothes and in his order of priorities Douglas put his wife's clothes after his children's education and a high enough standard of nourishment for the family. But it was becoming increasingly difficult. Fortunately there was complete understanding between husband and wife on the subject and Sheila never pressed her claims. But the days had long gone by when Douglas could tell her quite cheerfully to spend thirty or forty pounds on whatever she wanted in the way of a dress. But what would have cost thirty or forty pounds in those days would now cost seventy or eighty pounds or more.

One thing which Douglas had given up without telling Sheila was his club. Unlike most clubs today it was entirely a man's club and women were never admitted even to an annexe. Douglas decided that there was no sufficient justification for a subscription of eighty pounds a year spent on the luxury of a club which he did not use very often. Sheila would have refused to agree to his giving it up because she knew how much it meant to him. But, as she was never able to go to the club herself, it was easy for him to pretend that he had not resigned.

67

In fact when the subscription was raised to eighty pounds a year sixty members resigned, including Douglas.

But there was one thing on which the Bartons had to practise no economy. Like everyone else in the country, they could have it for nothing. Music. It is doubtful whether people sufficiently appreciate that on every day in the year they can hear on radio the most lovely music and they don't have to pay a penny for it. The introduction of the Third Programme by the B.B.C. was one of its finest achievements. It is perfectly true that at the moment comparatively few people listen to that programme, but there are in fact many thousands of them. Today with the popularity of television and the advent of pop music and the pop charts, the people concerned with the numbers of viewers talk in millions. But many thousands of people in fact constitute a considerable number and, apart from the enjoyment of these many people, there is the probability that, as the population as a whole is given more and more opportunity of becoming interested in good music, more people will listen to that programme. Even those responsible for the television programmes are aware of the value of music and sometimes produce programmes of outstanding excellence, for example the late quartets of Beethoven, to which nearly a week of evening television was devoted. This, of course, has to be paid for, though the cost of the television licence for black and white is small enough.

Sheila had never smoked but Douglas, who had been quite a heavy smoker, had given it up for about a year. He had also given up taking photographs, which was an expensive hobby. He had a fairly good library of classical records and a certain number of tape-recordings but he had not added to the library for over a year and did not intend to add to it any more. But in spite of their economies and their worries, particularly the fear that they might have to take the girls away from their school, they were an extremely happy family. Just as in a war there is far greater friendliness among the population in view of the perils and hardships which they have to share, so in a family which is normally happy, the necessary economies are accepted and, whenever possible, made the object of a joke, even a wry one.

Fortunately Douglas and Sheila and their children were all naturally happy people. Except in the event of tragedy or near-tragedy, a happy person remains happy and makes light of adversity. Conversely, the unhappy person will always find something to grumble about. And in fact the Bartons' situation was a very good one compared with a lot of other families, families who had no proper home, who had never enjoyed the luxuries which the Bartons had enjoyed and would have been delighted if their main problem was whether they would be able to keep their children at the same school.

But, though the Bartons were much better off than some people and much worse off than others, there was one thing which they had in common with the bulk of the population and that was the hope, however faint, of receiving a fortune which was round the corner, either in the shape of Douglas's premium bonds (of which he held a hundred) or Sheila's football pools. From time to time she would have Mitty-like dreams of receiving a telephone call from Vulgans, the big pool promoters, telling her that she had won half a million pounds. Then she would spend a minute or two in giving most of the money away and, when she had satisfactorily disposed of the bulk of her winnings, she got up and made the tea. Whether it is a good thing or a bad thing, the fact remains that taxation is so high that the only opportunity most people have of making a considerable sum of money is a win by gambling. The great advantage of the two forms of gambling indulged in by Douglas and Sheila was that, in Douglas's case, he only gambled with the interest and his capital remained, and, in Sheila's case, the amount which she had to spend each week to have the opportunity of a glorious win was so small that it was unnecessary to make it one of the economies of the household. Sometimes she wondered if, should she win the biggest prize

69

of all, Mr Vulgan would ring her up himself. She knew very little about the filling up of a football coupon but one thing which she did know was that you put a cross if you do not want publicity. She was always very careful to put that cross. She did not dare to think what would happen if everyone could know that she had won half a million pounds. But that would be better than not winning it at all.

CHAPTER SIX

Scooping the Pool

Edward appeared to settle down very well both with Theo and with Henry and Mrs Mountjoy. To such an extent did he appear to fit in that after about three weeks Theo told his parents that he had to go to the Midlands for the week-end and was proposing to leave Edward in charge unless they had any strong objections.

'Are you sure it's safe?'

'I'm pretty confident it is,' said Theo, 'but obviously no one can be sure of anything in a case like this. But I shall take care that he can't get at any of my secrets and he'd have some difficulty in making away with the whole of my stock during the week-end, while petty pilfering wouldn't be worth while. I think it should be all right, so long as you don't mind.'

'It's you we're thinking of,' said Douglas. 'If you're prepared to take the risk, so am I.'

'There is one thing,' said Theo. 'I wonder if you and Mum would let me have the car for the week-end? I've got to call at a number of places, so it would be tremendously helpful. I'd probably have to hire a car otherwise. But I could do that and, if you want it, I will.'

'I'll ask your mother,' said Douglas, 'but, as far as I'm concerned, certainly you can. We hardly use the car at all nowadays.'

Sheila was equally agreeable and on Friday morning Theo set off. Just before he left his mother said :

'You did remember to do my pools, I hope?'

'Oh yes.'

'And you did put the "no publicity" cross in?'

'The first thing I did.'

'Have a successful week-end and be careful how you drive.'

'See you Sunday night,' said Theo just before he drove away.

The week-end was uneventful for the Bartons. Douglas went down to the workshop to see how Edward was getting on and to keep an eye on him.

'How are you finding things?' he asked.

'Splendid,' said Edward. 'I couldn't be happier. Your son's a very clever young man, you know.'

'He's not too bad.'

'He's much more than that, I assure you. He's going to astonish you one day. And what a nice chap he is. I'd be very pleased to have a son like that.'

'Well, we are. How are you getting on next door?'

'That's fine too,' said Edward. 'The food's ever so much better than you get in prison and they're both very nice to me. Too nice, you might say. They treat me rather like people who have been given a death sentence by their doctor are treated by their friends. It's only natural, I suppose. And it's much nicer than if they made a point of locking up the spoons. They've got some quite nice silver, by the way. Don't worry,' he added. 'That's not in my line, though I do know a little about it.'

'D'you know exactly what Theo's doing this week-end? I know he's calling on customers, but is it just a routine call or something special?'

'It's just routine, I think, except that I believe he wants to unload rather a lot of radio components. He's made rather too many. He'll do it all right. That young man knows what he's about.'

On Sunday night Theo returned in time for supper. He said he'd had a successful trip but would have to go up again shortly, either the next week-end or the week-end after that, possibly both.

'By the way, Mum,' he asked at supper, 'did you look at the football results?'

'No. I never do. Why? Have I won a fortune?'

'Well, you've won a prize,' said Theo, 'but I wouldn't quite call it a fortune.'

'How much?'

'Just on two pounds.'

'You must bring me luck, Theo. I've never won anything before. That will pay for several weeks. Was it just luck or have you got some sort of a system?'

'Mostly luck,' said Theo, 'but I did put a certain amount of thought to it.'

In fact Theo went up again for the next three week-ends but on the Saturday night of the third week-end he telephoned his parents. Douglas answered the phone and noticed that Theo's voice appeared to be rather excited.

'Nothing the matter, I hope?' said his father.

'Oh dear no,' said Theo, 'but I want to prepare you for a surprise.'

'A nice one?'

'Yes, a very nice one.'

'What's it about?'

'Wait till I come home tomorrow. As a matter of fact, I'll be home a good bit earlier. Probably just after lunch. Don't have anybody else in. This is just between the three of us. For the moment anyway.'

'Has your mother won the pools or something?' asked Douglas.

'You'll see,' said Theo. 'Bye-bye.'

Although Sheila had been doing the pools for some time, she knew nothing whatever about them. She had never troubled to read the rules, she didn't look at the results of matches and had no idea what to do if she won a big prize. A large number of people who go in for pools do it in much the same way as Sheila. They no more look at the results of matches or listen to 'Final Score' than they study the numbers of prize-winning premium bonds. They take the view that they will be told soon enough if they've won anything. That certainly is so in the case of premium bonds. It looks as though the big pool promoters do not take advantage of the rule which requires successful entrants to make claims by telegram and registered letter. And sometimes by telephone. But there are such rules and the failure to observe them could result in a prize-winner being disqualified. However, from the fact that one hears of the representative of pool promoters calling on a house to announce to the surprised occupier that he has won a huge prize, there appears to be no rigid insistence upon compliance with the rules about claiming. But those who go in for pools should be careful not to be misled by this. People have been disqualified in the past by failure to fill in the coupon correctly, although it was quite plain what they intended by their entry.

Neither Douglas nor Sheila knew that there were any rules to comply with so far as claiming was concerned, but, as Theo had the copy of the coupon, they couldn't have found out what they were anyway. Unless of course they'd asked any of their friends and they wouldn't have dreamed of doing that in view of their desire, in the unlikely event of their having a big win, to keep the matter secret.

'We mustn't be too optimistic,' said Douglas. 'He hasn't said it was a pools win, though I must admit that I can't think what else he can be referring to. He says it's to be between the three of us and I could tell from his voice that he was very excited.'

'Well, we must be patient. But I must admit it would be marvellous if we won a few thousand pounds.'

Douglas slept well that night but Sheila hardly slept at all and, when she did, she had such extraordinary dreams that she was quite glad to wake up.

Shortly after lunch on the Sunday they heard the car arriving and they were on the doorstep to greet Theo. As soon as he came in he told them.

'We've done it,' he said. 'We've got a first dividend.'

'What does that mean?' asked Douglas. 'I suppose it depends on how many other people have got a first dividend too.'

'Yes, indeed,' said Theo, 'and that depends upon how many score-draws there were.'

'What's a score-draw?' asked Sheila.

'A draw where each side scores something. It could be 1–1, 2–2, 3–3, or anything you like so long as they score. They introduced that in order to make a bigger first dividend, because, when goalless draws were included, there were often too many draws.'

'How many draws were there this week? Score-draws, I mean,' asked Douglas.

'There were eight,' said Theo. 'Just eight.'

'What'll that mean?'

'Well, no one can be sure, but I'd be very surprised if you got less than a hundred thousand pounds.'

'What?' exclaimed both of his parents. 'D'you mean that?'

'Of course I do. You may even have scooped the pool and got half a million.'

'I can't believe it,' said Sheila.

'There's only one thing,' said Theo.

'What's that?'

'Let's hope they received the coupon. I posted it all right but that doesn't mean they're bound to have got it. I expect they have though. You've got to get busy. First of all you've got to send a telegram. I should do it by telephone.'

'What have we got to say on it?'

'It will read like this. "Mrs Sheila Barton, Old Cottage, Sycamore Lane, Redhill, Surrey, claims 24 points on Treble

75

Chance for the 31st May 1975. Reference No. 72816." I think you might add your telephone number too, because I read that they sometimes ring you up and confirm that your entry's in order. Then first thing on Monday you'll have to send a registered letter confirming your claim, but I expect you'll have heard from them before that. Now there's one thing I must warn you about. I put a cross in the no publicity box but naturally pool promoters prefer to be able to advertise widely the big wins. Publicity is of course good for them and, if you have scooped the pool, they would love to give you lunch at the Savoy and have a picture of some well-known actress presenting you with a cheque.'

'But they can't do that,' said Douglas, 'as we've asked for no publicity.'

'The point is,' said Theo, 'that they will want to do it. Now there's no legal contract between you and the pool promoters. They're not even legally liable to pay you. Of course they always do. Similarly they're not legally liable to refrain from giving you publicity, but, if you've asked for no publicity and don't go back on that, they'll keep their word and you won't get any. But what they will do is to try as hard as they possibly can to persuade you to waive your little cross in the box. I saw it stated the other day that a substantial proportion of the people who've asked for no publicity eventually yield and agree to it. Now you've got to dig your heels in. Do it very nicely, of course. You don't want to annoy them, though you quite understand their point of view. Tell them you're very sorry but you're definitely not prepared to agree to it. In the end, if you're firm, they'll accept your decision.'

'How is it you know so much about pools, Theo?' asked Douglas. 'You've never done them yourself, have you?'

'Good gracious no,' said Theo. 'But when I said I'd do Mum's for her, I thought I'd better learn something about them, so I made a lot of enquiries and they seem to have paid off.'

76

The telegram was duly sent and on Monday morning at nine o'clock Theo was at Redhill Post Office to post his mother's claim by registered letter.

Just after Douglas returned home on Tuesday evening the telephone rang and Sheila answered it.

'This is Vulgans Pools here. May I speak to Mrs Sheila Barton?'

'Speaking.'

'We have your telegram and letter and are glad to say that your claim is in order. So far we've had no other claim and, if none comes along, you should receive half a million pounds. I should like to congratulate you.'

'Thank you very much.'

'My name is Hopkins. If there's no other claim, I'll ring to let you know about the presentation of the cheque. We hope that Ruby Sweetenham will be available but we're not quite sure at the moment.'

'But I don't quite understand. I asked for no publicity.'

'I'm afraid you didn't,' said Mr Hopkins.

Sheila put her hand over the mouthpiece and whispered to Douglas: 'You'd better speak to him. He says I didn't ask for no publicity.'

Douglas took the receiver. 'Forgive me interrupting,' he said, 'but I'm Mrs Barton's husband and I don't quite understand about this publicity business.'

'The position is simply that you didn't ask for no publicity, or rather your wife didn't.'

'But she did. I'm sure she did.'

'Quite definitely she did not. I have the coupon in front of me and I'll send you a photostat copy. There is no cross in the box. If she didn't want any publicity she should have put one. If she had, we would have honoured her request. I may say that she was able to put eight crosses in the right places in the other part of the coupon, so she should have been able to put one cross in that part.'

77

'Can't you treat the matter as though she had?'

'I'm afraid we can't. As I'm sure you will realise, Mr Barton, the publicity means a great deal to us. If your wife wins half a million pounds, as I hope she will, she will be one of under twenty people who've had such a big win. This is very important from a pool promoter's point of view. I am sure you will see that.'

'Yes, I can. But I'm sure you can see our point of view.'

'I do, but as your wife didn't put a cross, I'm afraid she must take the consequences. I may tell you that, if she had put a cross, I should have done my best to argue her out of it. Usually I succeed in persuading people, but, if I don't, I have to accept their refusal, just as I'm afraid you will have to accept ours.'

'You can't make us come to the Savoy and receive a cheque from an actress, can you?'

'Of course we can't, but as a sensible man I'm sure you will realise that it's in your wife's interest and your own to do what we suggest. You see, we're entitled to give you all the publicity we want. We can send photographers to snap you when you leave your house or when you're walking in the street. We shall certainly give your name and address to the B.B.C. and the television companies and they're sure to do something about it. You can, of course, refuse to answer any questions that you're asked, but, if you do that, it will only look as if you're rather disagreeable people, and the whole world will know who you are and where you live and what you look like, whatever you do or refuse to do. Please don't think that I'm trying to threaten you. I am merely telling you the facts, and I can assure you that you will find it much more pleasant and much easier if you go along with us. As a matter of fact, you should find it very pleasant. We have a private room and you will get a very good lunch. Everybody will be very happy and cheerful and you will only have to submit to the taking of a few photographs. As we can get your photographs anyway, won't it be more sensible to relax and enjoy it? By the way, how many children have you?'

'Three.'

'Well, they'll like it for sure.'

'Two of them are at school and won't get the chance. There will be enough stir at the school anyway. We shall all be surrounded by people who want to go shares. Now don't get me wrong. A large number of people and charities will have a share. That will be one of the pleasures of having the money. But it's a very different thing to give away money to people or causes which you know are deserving from being bombarded by cadgers and beggars and criminals.'

'So far as that's concerned,' said Mr Hopkins, 'we'll do the best we can to help you. While we don't want to interfere in the least, we'll be only too glad to make available to you a very experienced man on our staff who knows all about that sort of thing. He can advise you which letters to ignore, which to reply to and which to take to the police.'

'Well,' said Douglas, 'thank you very much for the offer. I'll let you know if we want to take advantage of it. Now I must talk about this to my wife and to my son, but I realise that you may be right and that, as my wife made a mistake, it may be better to fall in with your suggestions.'

'If I may say so, that's a very sensible way of taking it. I'm extremely sorry for the mistake, but, as it was your wife's, I'm afraid we must hold you to it. Having said that, I can assure you that everything will be done as pleasantly as possible and, if you will all co-operate, we will consult with you fully as to the form of the publicity. Of course we can't be absolutely certain that another claim won't come in, but, even if it does, your wife will have a very large win indeed.'

Douglas said goodbye and replaced the receiver. 'There was nothing else I could do,' he said to Sheila, 'but it's a damned nuisance.'

When Theo came home that evening he couldn't believe

that he had made a mistake and forgotten to put in the cross.

'You remember, Mum,' he said, 'you particularly asked me not to forget to put it. And I actually thought of your saying that when I put it. I simply can't understand it.'

'D'you think they could have rubbed it off?' said Douglas. 'Publicity means so much to them.'

'I don't think they'd do that,' said Theo. 'It would be bound to show. You'd probably be able to see where the surface had been roughened, even without a microscope. Whatever people may say about bookmakers and pool promoters, I don't think they'd do a thing like that. It's absolutely beyond me. It must be my fault and I'm terribly sorry. I really have let you in for it.'

'You've also let us in for half a million pounds or something like it,' said Sheila. 'So I don't think we ought to feel too angry with you.'

Early next morning the Bartons received another call from Vulgans. Another representative spoke to Sheila.

'I'm glad to tell you, Mrs Barton,' he said, 'that there are no further claims and the time has now expired for further claims to be made. If any legitimate claim came in late, we would honour it, but it would have to come in very soon. Mr Reynolds is on his way now to come and see you and he is bringing with him the original coupon so that you can see in fact that no cross was put in the no publicity box. He will ring up when he gets to London and I expect he will be with you at about twelve o'clock.'

'Can he come to lunch?' asked Sheila.

'I'm sure he'd be very pleased.'

As soon as the telephone conversation was over, Sheila telephoned Douglas at his library.

'D'you think it's possible for you to come back to lunch?' she said. 'I know you don't like taking a half day, but this man's coming to see us and producing the coupon and you'd be much better at dealing with him than me. And you should be able to get out of him when our name's likely to be published. We must discuss how to deal with it.'

'All right,' said Douglas. 'I'll come back. What are you going to give him for lunch? You'd better do him well, hadn't you?'

'I'll go into Redhill and get some smoked salmon.'

'And you'd better get a couple of bottles of champagne too. I hate the stuff, but the gentleman will probably like it and expect it of us. By the way, does Edward know what's happened?'

'Not yet.'

'Well, don't ask him to lunch. Send him back to Henry.'

'I'd thought of that,' said Sheila. 'Nothing else you want to say in case he comes before you get back?'

'I don't think so, except don't agree to anything until I'm there. You can always say you've got to consult me first.'

'All right,' said Sheila. 'Now I must be off if I'm going to make a decent lunch.'

'It will be a change, won't it. How long is it since we had smoked salmon?'

CHAPTER SEVEN

Breaking the News

Douglas was able to get back home before the representative of Vulgans Pools arrived. So he and Sheila were able to greet Mr Reynolds together.

'My first duty,' said Mr Reynolds, 'is to congratulate you both on behalf of Vulgans Pools. The management wishes me to extend to you their very best wishes for every happiness in the future. That's the official announcement. Privately, I offer you my condolences. But I hope you won't repeat that to my employers or I'll get the sack. I'm one of the few people with a conscience and I should feel I'd be letting myself down if I didn't tell you how very sorry I was for you.'

'It's very kind of you,' said Douglas, 'but I hope there won't be any need for it.'

'Don't you believe it,' said Mr Reynolds. 'There'll be every need for it. Now please don't think I'm suggesting you'll be like one or two of our winners and take to drink or drugs or gambling or go to the bad morally and physically. It isn't necessary to do any of those things in order to be miserable.'

'Before you go any further,' said Douglas, 'would you care for a drink?'

'I should be delighted,' said Mr Reynolds. 'But I should warn you that drink has no uplifting effect on me. If anything, it makes me feel depressed. But I am the person at fault. From time to time I've said that every job I've had was depressing. I was a telegraph boy once, nearly always bringing bad news even if it was wrapped up in one of the Post Office's greetings forms. D'you know that one in seven marriages now ends in divorce? I've sent those telegrams myself. "Wish you every conceivable happiness. I'm sure you will have it," I used to say. The next thing I knew was that both sides were consulting me as to how to get a divorce quickest. I sold cars once. That's a depressing job, isn't it? A lovely brand new car and you know perfectly well that, if it isn't the ignition that's going to fail it will be the petrol-feed or the brakes or the gears or the clutch or the radiator will leak. Indeed there's so much that can go wrong with a car it's surprising you see so many actually moving. But I mustn't talk about my own troubles.'

'Would you like a glass of champagne?' said Sheila. 'Or do you prefer sherry or whisky or gin?'

'That's another of the crosses I have to bear,' said Mr Reynolds. 'I'm always offered champagne. I hate the stuff, but most prize-winners expect me to drink it.'

'We certainly don't,' said Douglas. 'We hate the stuff too.'

At that moment Henry arrived.

'I'm awfully sorry, Henry,' said Sheila, 'but this is a confidential interview. Would you come back a little later?'

'Of course,' said Henry. 'I'll just have a quick one and be gone. You won't see me for dust. Champagne, is it?'

'As a matter of fact, we weren't going to open it.'

'Now I've given you an excuse,' said Henry. 'I say, Krug 1961. Aren't you going it a bit? That must have cost you five quid a bottle. How d'you do,' he said to Mr Reynolds. 'My name's Henry Bunting.'

'How d'you do. Mine is Blanco Reynolds.'

'My father used to know a Blanco White. No relation, I suppose?'

'No,' said Mr Reynolds. 'I was christened Blanco by accident.

83

The parson was absent-minded and deaf. That wouldn't have mattered so much but he poured the water all over me.'

'You actually remember being christened?' said Henry.

'As a matter of fact,' said Mr Reynolds, 'I remember being born.'

'What did it feel like?'

'Horrible. I never forgave my father or mother. Have you ever seen a baby being born? If you have, how would you like it? It happened to you as a matter of fact.'

'It did happen to me,' said Henry, 'but I expect they gave me twilight sleep or something. You could have had that, you know.'

'Not for a christening.'

'Henry,' said Douglas, 'Mr Reynolds has something rather important to discuss with us and, as it's confidential, I would be grateful if you'd disappear. You can have a drink with us later.'

'I tell you what,' said Henry, 'if none of you likes the idea of champagne – you all seem to be drinking something else – I could relieve you of it. Mrs Mountjoy and I could share it. It would be a pity to waste it.'

'I expect Theo would like a glass,' said Sheila.

'Certainly,' said Henry. 'I might save one for him. Tell him to come round when he gets home. I won't keep you any more.' And, picking up the bottle, Henry left.

'That's nothing,' said Mr Reynolds. 'Just you wait. You've no idea what's going to happen to you.'

'Do come in and sit down,' said Sheila.

'Thank you.'

They went into the sitting room.

'Now,' said Mr Reynolds, 'it's my duty to inform you that you've won half a million pounds and that tomorrow the cheque will be presented to you by the film actress Dulcie Mainwaring. They tried to get Ruby Sweetenham but she couldn't manage it. I'm told you didn't want any publicity.'

'That's quite true,' said Douglas. 'I suppose it's too late to arrange that.'

'Oh much too late,' said Mr Reynolds. 'But that's about the only good news I can give to you. You wanted the whole thing kept secret. Well, it couldn't have been. In the first place, you had to send a telegram, didn't you? Whether you sent it by telephone or over the counter it would be very difficult for the person who took it not to spread the good news around. Then you've got to pay the cheque into your bank somehow. I know that bank managers and bank cashiers are all taught to treat their clients' business in confidence and for the most part they do. But how can you expect a bank cashier who's given half a million pounds, the proceeds of a football pool win, to pay into a client's account not to mention it to his wife? And then friends. What about your friend Mr Bunting who has just left us? He must think something very queer's going on. He'll soon find out. The more secret you try to keep it, the more interest it creates. I'm bound to say we keep our word absolutely. If you'd put the little cross in the right place on the coupon and we couldn't persuade you to waive it, not a word would go out from our office. No, *you'd* be the people who spread the news, however unwillingly. And then, if you're like most people, you'll want to give a lot of it away. Either you'll tell the people you give it to where you got the money from or you won't. If you do, you'll certainly spread the news and equally if you don't. Because they'll guess. "Must have won a football pool or something," they'll say. If that's any comfort to you – and by jove you're going to need some comfort badly – you needn't feel too worried that you didn't put in the little cross.'

'It's very nice of you to try and console us,' said Douglas.

'But surely,' said Sheila, 'you've had winners who've been able to improve their lives and do things they couldn't possibly have done without the money.'

'Of course. I didn't say you wouldn't improve your lives.

85

You can have six cars instead of one or two if you like. And a fat lot of good that'll do you. You could dine at the Caprice every night if it hadn't closed down. You won't have to worry where the money's going to come from to pay the next rate demand. I didn't say there weren't things on the plus side. Of course there are. But by the time you prepare your balance sheet, say at the end of five years if you're like most other people, you'll wish it had never happened.'

'Let me fill your glass,' said Douglas.

'Thank you,' said Mr Reynolds. 'A very nice sherry, if I may say so.'

'Tell us some of the terrible things that are going to happen to us,' said Douglas.

'To start with, there'll be the begging letters. Now, if you're selfish, uncompassionate people, not in the least sensitive, and don't care two hoots what happens to other people, they won't worry you so much. But, if I may say so, from the way you let your neighbour take away that bottle of champagne, those are the last adjectives that could be said of you. I don't think there are many people who could have got away with that. You are going to have not tens or hundreds but thousands of begging letters. Some of them will tell the truth. Some of them will tell lies as though they were the truth. And you won't be able to refuse one request without wondering whether some poor chap living on a small pension and looking after an invalid wife and two invalid parents shouldn't have been given some help. You'll imagine him sending off the letter and wondering when it would reach you and how soon you'll be able to reply and whether the reply will come at all and, if it does come, whether it will contain some money. You will imagine him thinking about the posts, particularly today. He will actually spend sevenpence on his letter to you, which he could not really afford. That's to say he can't afford it if it's a genuine letter. Now you may say – and your friends will certainly say – that the really genuine people don't ask. Well, it's quite true that most of them don't. But there are a few, a very few, who feel they're bound to. This chap who's not able to look after his sick wife in the way that he would like to do because he's got to spread his slender means over his elderly parents as well, is reduced to begging from you by sheer necessity. Oh, he's able to give them enough to eat and to keep them warm. But he wants to be able to give his wife some luxuries and without help he can't. So he sees that you've won half a million pounds. How can it hurt you to give away a couple of hundred? It would mean nothing to you and everything to him so he feels he's got a duty to ask you for it. In nine cases out of ten his parents died years ago and his wife is hale and hearty. But you can't go investigating each case yourself or you'd be doing nothing else. So you'll either have to employ snoopers to go all over the country and make enquiries or you'll have to refuse or give way. Now you won't like employing snoopers, because you won't know them and you won't know the way they'll treat the people who've written the letters. If you're kindly people, you won't want to add to the unhappiness of the man with the sick wife and the elderly parents when he suddenly finds a private detective asking him leading questions in an offensive tone. I don't mean that all private detectives are like that, but you won't know. Of course you can accede to every demand that's made on you and, if you do that, by the time you've finished you'll probably have spent the lot.'

'This is a very different interview from what I'd expected,' said Sheila.

'Oh, I can turn on the other tap,' said Mr Reynolds, 'if you'd like me to. My dear Mr and Mrs Barton, what a happy moment this is for you and for me. I'm delighted to be the bringer of such good tidings to you. Now you'll be in a position to do all the things that you've wanted to do and so far have been prevented by lack of funds. Never in your lives again will you be short of a penny. What a happy prospect. What a lot of good you'll be able to do with the money. Giving money to charity in a way which you would have liked to do in the past but have been prevented by the heavy drain on your income. Giving money to friends who need it even more than you do. What a delightful prospect. Your very good health.'

'And yours,' said Douglas.

'Thank you,' said Mr Reynolds, 'but I didn't really mean it. I was only giving you the other side of the coin. Let me go on. You have children, no doubt. If they're young enough still to require educating you'll be able to give them all the education they need and assist them to start a career in any sphere that they want.'

'As a matter of fact,' said Sheila, 'knowing that we shall be able to look after our children properly will be a great joy to us.'

'I was afraid of that,' said Mr Reynolds. 'Let me tell you the truth. I'm intensely jealous of you. That's what it really is. Just think what it must be like for me to go round giving people the news that they've won hundreds of thousands of pounds or at any rate fifty thousand or so. I'm paid less than a hard-working bricklayer. It's enough to make anybody jealous. And it's not as though you've earned the money. I expect you did it with a pin. And, if you didn't, you could do as well with a pin. Now a man who's discovered a cure for cancer is *worth* half a million pounds or more.'

'May I ask why you do the job?' said Douglas.

'Why indeed?' said Mr Reynolds. 'As a matter of fact I was in the security department and then they asked me if I'd like a change and offered me a small rise. I accepted and here I am. The only fun I get out of the job is talking like this, wondering how you'll take it and seeing the surprise on your faces. And it's not often I can do this. Most people wouldn't understand and might report me to my employers. If they didn't do it deliberately, it would slip out. So you needn't take it too much to heart. What I've said about begging letters is very true, but you'll find a way of coping with them.'

'Might I ask you a question?' said Douglas. 'Is it against the rules of your firm to offer you a present? We would be very pleased if we were allowed to do so.'

'I'm afraid it is,' said Mr Reynolds.

'That seems a bit hard,' said Douglas. 'It would give us a lot of pleasure to know that you could share in our good fortune. And I expect a lot of prize-winners feel the same.'

'Yes,' said Mr Reynolds. 'But the trouble is that it would be so easy for me or anybody in my position to get it out of you in one way or another and that would give the firm a bad name.'

'I see that,' said Douglas. 'But I shall ask your manager or one of your directors or whoever the right person is to ask whether we can give you five hundred pounds. I'll say that it would give us a great deal of pleasure to do so and assure him that the suggestion came entirely from us and was not in the least prompted by you, either directly or indirectly.'

'That's very, very kind of you and, whether my boss allows it or not, I very much appreciate the gesture. If you're like that with me, heaven help you when you come to deal with the begging letters. Your hearts will need a good deal more steel in them than they appear to have.'

At that moment Theo came into the room. 'Any chance of lunch?' he said. 'Oh, I'm sorry. I didn't realise you had a guest.'

'This is my son Theodore,' said Douglas. 'This is Mr Reynolds from Vulgans Pools. He's come to tell us that your mother's won half a million pounds.'

'I must say you all look very miserable on the strength of it,' said Theo. 'May I take a glass of sherry?'

'Of course. As a matter of fact it was Theo who filled in the coupon for me,' said Sheila.

'Any particular system?'

'My own,' said Theo. 'But it's quite a simple one. To disregard most of the advice given by the tipsters. Obviously a lot of people follow them and, if you do too and win, the probability is that a lot of others will win too.'

'Congratulations anyway,' said Mr Reynolds. 'And may I ask if you are entitled to half the prize?'

'No,' said Theo. 'I'm not entitled to any of it. I gave my services to my mother for love.'

'You'll certainly have to be there when Miss Dulcie Mainwaring presents the cheque. You'll probably be allowed to give her a kiss. As you're nearly twenty years younger than she is, she'll be very pleased I've no doubt. May I ask if you've stayed at home especially to meet me?'

'Oh no,' said Theo. 'I work here. My premises are at the bottom of the garden. I make electronic equipment and that sort of thing.'

'Indeed?' said Mr Reynolds. 'You should be able to spread yourself now.'

'Don't you believe it,' said Theo. 'That's asking for trouble.'

At that moment the telephone rang and Douglas answered it. A voice at the other end said he wanted to speak to Mr Reynolds. Douglas handed him the receiver.

'Reynolds here,' he said. 'Yes. Yes. Oh yes. I quite understand. Thanks very much.'

'They've just rung up to say they've had another claim which, if confirmed, will result in yours being halved. I hope you'll be able to manage on a quarter of a million, but between you and me I don't think you'll have to.'

'A quarter of a million should just do,' said Theo. 'But why don't you think that my mother will have to put up with such a miserable pittance?'

'It looks as though the other claim is not a genuine one.'

'Fraudulent, d'you mean?' said Douglas.

'As you don't know the name of the claimants, it doesn't matter my saying so. Yes, fraudulent. We do get a few of those. But not as many as you might think considering how much is at stake.'

'When will you know about this claim?' asked Douglas.

'We'll know within twenty-four hours whether it's a genuine

one. It will take rather longer to know whether a charge of fraud can be made.'

'How much would a chap get for fraud of this kind?' asked Theo.

'It depends whether he'd got any previous convictions,' said Reynolds. 'It also depends how deliberate a plan he made. The most serious of these frauds are when there's a conspiracy between somebody outside and somebody inside. If it's one of those, they get about three years, I think, for a first offence. You see,' he explained, 'this is what I used to do when I was on the security side.'

'You mean, I suppose,' said Theo, 'that somebody outside arranges to have his coupon filled in and inserted as a genuine coupon as soon as the results of the matches are known?'

'Something of that kind,' said Mr Reynolds.

'What other fraudulent ways are there of winning?' asked Douglas.

'Postmarks is the normal one. A very simple kind is when a person sends a letter to himself a day before the matches putting the name and address in pencil pretty lightly. When he receives the letter he then rubs out the pencil and inserts our name and address instead. Then on the same day he drops the letter in our letter box. That's a pretty foolish kind of fraud but they try it on from time to time. You see, in the first place, if the coupon is sent in anything but our printed envelope, it's suspicious. So it gets examined extremely carefully and of course, if you pass a rubber over paper, there are bound to be traces where it's been roughed up.'

'What happens in those cases?' asked Theo.

'When I was in the security department, sometimes one of my colleagues would go and interview the claimant and ask him a few questions. The first question is why he hadn't used the ordinary envelope. Oh, that's been torn or thrown away or something of that sort. Sometimes after that I can show him a photostat copy of the envelope with the actual indentation of

91

his own name and address on it. After that he usually caves in and admits it. But some chaps are very brazen. Then we put the police on to it.'

'D'you often prosecute?' asked Theo.

'We usually leave that to the police, but in a bad case they always do. But, you see, another trouble for the chaps who try that stupid fraud on is that the letter arrives in our office after the matches have been played and not with the ordinary post. What's the explanation of that? Of course we have had cases of dishonest postmen and naturally they always prosecute in those cases.'

'D'you happen to know where the man who has made the other claim lives?' Not in this area, I suppose.'

'It would be a very odd coincidence if it were,' said Mr Reynolds.

'Where's Edward, by the way?' asked Douglas.

'He's gone back to Henry for lunch.'

'D'you know if he likes champagne?'

'I haven't the faintest idea.'

'Perhaps they'll be offering him a glass.'

'How d'you know?'

'Because Henry pinched the bottle from us.'

CHAPTER EIGHT

The Problem of Sudden Wealth

The lunch passed off uneventfully and Mr Reynolds left, but he telephoned the same evening to say that the other claim was not confirmed. It was not a fraudulent claim but it was due to a mistake. The claimant had not kept a proper copy of his coupon and he had only got seven score-draws.

After supper that evening the Bartons received a visit from Mrs Mountjoy. She apologised profusely for troubling them.

'I'm very sorry to bother you,' she said after they had asked her in and she was sitting down, 'and I hope you don't think I'm interfering. But it's about my guv'nor.'

'Henry, d'you mean?' asked Sheila.

'That's what you call him. I do hope you won't think I'm interfering but I'm afraid I had to come. I want to ask you a favour.'

'Of course, if we can help.'

'It's just this. I know you're very kind to him and I wouldn't want to stop that, but I must please ask you not to give him any more bottles of champagne. I don't like the stuff, he drank the lot and was sick as a dog. I shouldn't so much have minded if he'd done it in the proper place, even though he made an awful noise about it. But he did it all over my new settee and that really is not good enough. I've known him the worse for wear before but normally he can hold his drink pretty well.

Between you and me he doesn't often have very much to hold. Probably that's the reason why a whole bottle of champagne was too much for him. But he's never done it before and I wanted to make sure it doesn't happen again. I do hope you'll forgive me.'

'Of course,' said Sheila. 'You must let us know what it costs to have the settee cleaned or re-covered if necessary.'

'That wasn't why I came.'

'Of course it wasn't. But we'd like to do it and it would make us feel happier. I'm sure that Douglas agrees with me. We feel in a way responsible. We'd no idea that he'd drink it all himself. As a matter of fact he promised to keep a glass of it for Theo because Douglas and I don't like it.'

'That's a good thing,' said Mrs Mountjoy. 'So you won't be having any more.'

'We might have some for our friends but we won't give Henry a whole bottle to take away.'

'As a matter of fact,' said Douglas, 'we didn't give it him. He took it.'

'He stole it, d'you mean?'

'Oh no. He picked it up and we didn't try and stop him or tell him he wasn't to, so no doubt he thought we were consenting. But in view of what's happened I'm very sorry we did.'

'It's very nice of you to take it like that. But I wouldn't dream of letting you pay for it. I'm sure it will clean and I will give the bill to the guv'nor.'

'If he makes a fuss about it,' said Douglas, 'do send it on to us.'

'If he makes a fuss,' said Mrs Mountjoy, 'I'll tell him what he can do with his fuss. He can stuff it.'

Douglas and Sheila had not previously heard Mrs Mountjoy using her vernacular, and the contrast between the words she used and the way she used them was so great that they were reduced to shocked silence. Mrs Mountjoy must have noticed it because she said : 'Have I said something?'

'Oh not at all,' said Sheila. 'Would you care for a glass of sherry or something?'

'That would be very kind.'

'I'm afraid it's British at the moment but I hope that the next time you come we shall be able to give you something better.'

'I'm British,' said Mrs Mountjoy, 'and bloody proud of it.'

'Of course,' said Douglas, and he poured her out a glass of sherry. She raised it to her lips, sipped it and then said :

'Bung ho.'

Sheila, remembering King Edward VII and the finger bowls, repeated the phrase for the first time in her life. Douglas, rather sheepishly, followed suit.

Mrs Mountjoy put down her glass. 'I see what you mean. Well, we can't have everything and no one will ever beat us for brains. That young son of yours at the bottom of the garden. He's a bright young man. Did he really make those aeroplanes himself?'

'He certainly did,' said Douglas.

'What's he inventing now?' asked Mrs Mountjoy.

'He's always doing something,' said Sheila, 'but I have an idea he's on to something spectacular.'

'Now, Sheila, we mustn't say anything at the moment. If too many people knew about it we might get some industrial spies down here.'

'I won't say a bloody word,' said Mrs Mountjoy. She left half an hour later without finishing her sherry.

'That was most illuminating,' said Douglas.

'Illuminating?'

'Yes. How much d'you think it would cost to re-cover her new sofa?'

'It might be all of fifty pounds. To clean it would probably cost nine or ten.'

'And here we are offering to do one or the other when forty-eight hours ago we couldn't have afforded to have offered anything. It shows how quickly one gets into the habit. But I tell you one thing,' he went on, 'we'd better wait until we actually get the cheque and have it cleared. As Theo told us, there's nothing legally binding about the pools and, although I'm quite sure they will pay us, they can't be forced to do so. Supposing we lost our heads and bought a lot of things and the pools company went bust and didn't pay us anything, we'd look a bit silly. So that little visit of Mrs Mountjoy was quite useful.'

'But shouldn't I get a new dress for the presentation?' said Sheila.

Douglas went through the motion of shivering. 'Oh Lord, there's that to come. I suppose you'll have to. What blithering idiots we shall look. I can't bear the thought of it. And then he says we're likely to be interviewed on Nationwide or something of that sort. I thought that a jolly good programme till now. We'd better make up our minds about what we're going to say when we're asked the questions they're bound to ask us. How did we feel when we heard we'd won half a million pounds? Is it going to change our way of life? What are we going to do with the money? Are we going to buy a Rolls-Royce? Are we going to change our house? Can you think of any others, Sheila?'

'I suppose they might ask me if I'm going to change my dressmaker, to which I can truthfully say No, because I haven't got one.'

'I shouldn't worry very much about the truth,' said Douglas.

'I'm sure it will be easier,' said Sheila.

'It won't be very interesting,' said Douglas. 'What we both felt when we heard we'd won half a million pounds. It was "Thank heaven for that. Now we can pay the school fees." We shan't change our way of life except that we shall be able to live better than we have in the last few months. I shan't give up my job.'

'Have you any particular causes that you want to support now that you can afford to do it in a big way?' said Sheila.

'I suppose the answer to that is Yes, there are several, and, when they ask me would I mind saying what they are, I'll answer that I think perhaps I'd better not, in case I disappointed any of them. I suppose that they will then ask us if we're going to celebrate that evening. I tell you what we will do, by the way. The three of us will drink that bottle of claret. We can always get some more.'

'Don't you feel rather ashamed of saying that?' said Sheila. 'It will probably cost you ten or twenty pounds a bottle to buy some more and that bottle cost us about a pound.'

'You're quite right,' said Douglas. 'But if we handed the whole of it over to the Government it wouldn't increase the old age pension by sixpence. Nonetheless, when one thinks of people who really are badly off, it does feel a bit awkward splashing around and paying a hundred or two for a dozen bottles of wine. As, by the way, I certainly shall. What's going to be your first extravagance?'

'To try and find someone who can really do my hair,' said Sheila. 'And when I've found her, I shall grossly overtip her and try to make certain that I shall always get an appointment when I want it.'

'Oh, another thing,' said Douglas. 'We shall be asked whether we want to go round the world. Do you?'

'Not in the least,' said Sheila. 'I'm very happy with this part of it, but if you wanted to go, I'd come with you.'

'I should hate it,' said Douglas. 'But we'll have to decide what to do with the money. What to keep, I mean. First of all we'll put it on deposit and that'll give us time to think about it. And we'll have to consult solicitors and accountants because of all the legislation that's going around, wealth tax, transfer tax and heaven only knows what else. We'll find we have to pay all of it to the Government if we're not careful.'

'I wonder what Theo will want to do?'

'I shouldn't be surprised if he won't take any of it at all.'

'Why on earth not?'

'He's very anxious to prove to himself that he can get on

without anybody else's help. What Theo's doing is building up a business, little by little and in his own way. He knows exactly what's happening and exactly how much he owes and exactly how much is coming in and exactly what materials he needs and exactly what orders he's got to fill. Once he had large premises and large numbers of employees much of that would be out of his hands. I may be wrong and he may want to try and I shan't think any the worse of him if he does, but that's my feeling.'

'If he gets married in the next year or two, surely he'll let us buy him a house and give him something to make sure that he can keep a wife and family?'

'It's possible but I rather doubt it. Of course he can always know that he can fall back on us if he gets into difficulties.'

'Well,' said Sheila, 'I'm going to buy him a car whether he likes it or not. And whether you like it or not. Good gracious. I never thought of that. It's *my* money.'

'Of course it is. I shall be most grateful for anything that may come my way. A pair of really good binoculars, for instance. One that I can really see the birds with.'

'You shall have them – with the claret, which you'll need the money for. No, seriously. I suggest that we each have £5,000 in our current account to enjoy ourselves with.'

'I shan't want £5,000,' said Douglas. 'I wouldn't know what to do with it.'

'Well I shall. Now about the girls. We'll have their rooms redecorated and put a new tape recorder in each.'

'That's O.K., but we want to be sure that they don't get spoiled.'

'I'm going to spoil them as much as I like. For years we've had to say No to this and No to that and during the last year it's been No to everything except a tooth-brush. Now we're going to enjoy ourselves and they're going to enjoy themselves. And if they haven't got enough character in them from me not to be ruined by it, it will be your fault. And I'm going to spoil you too. And myself.'

'You must be careful they don't get laughed at at school with all their new found wealth.'

'Laughed at! I seem to remember your telling me that your father once found half a sovereign after the school sports. He was ten at the time. D'you remember what happened? He gave it to the headmaster and, as no one claimed it, the head-master gave it back to him. He had no money at the time and what did he do with the half sovereign? Took all his friends along to the tuck shop and spent the lot. We won't let them overdo it and I'll tell them to speak to Miss Webster before they do anything really silly. We'd better ring her up by the way, I suppose, and tell her about it in confidence. We must certainly let her know before the news breaks.'

'I quite agree,' said Douglas, 'but I ought to remind you that no one on my side of the family has ever gone bankrupt.'

'Uncle Theo doesn't count. They always say he did it to help a friend. And, by the way, if this win hadn't come along you might have gone bankrupt yourself or you'd have had to take the children away from school.'

'I'm glad we haven't got to.'

'Where shall I get my new dress?'

'You know that better than I do, but you'll have to hurry. There won't be time to make it and it'll probably need altera-tions if you buy it off the peg and you'll want it by Wednesday or Thursday.'

'What a pity. I'd love to go to that little woman who made me a dress for twelve pounds last year. Nothing could have fitted me better.'

'I agree. You look lovely in it. Why not settle for that and not bother about a new one?'

'A jolly good idea. It was you who suggested a new one. That will save me one journey up to town.'

'You can have as many new dresses afterwards as you want.'

'I shan't want all that number. But what I would like is a

really nice winter coat. I don't want a very expensive one. Mink or anything like that. But something that looks nice and is really warm. Something I've never been able to buy. That would be fun. After I've got my hairdresser I think I'll go for that.'

'I tell you another thing. You'll be able to have some domestic help here, whether you like it or not.'

'I enjoy it in the kitchen. I should hate somebody else cooking all your meals.'

'That's all right. If you want to do the cooking, you certainly can. But the cleaning's going to be done by somebody else. And that's going to start next week as soon as the cheque is cleared. Out of my five thousand, if you like.'

'All right. Cleaning if you like, but I'm going on mending your clothes. I enjoy it.'

'Certainly,' said Douglas. 'That's fair enough, but I think you've put your finger on the spot. Just because we can afford to live anywhere we like, we're not going to give up any of the things we enjoy doing. I tell you what. We haven't been out for dinner for years. On Friday let's go to that little place we used to love to go to. It was quite cheap in the old days, and, if the standard's still the same, we shall enjoy it.'

'Don't forget, Douglas, he'll know who we are.'

'He knows already.'

'I mean he'll have seen us on television.'

'Oh hell. Everyone will have seen us on television. Or nearly everyone. As far as that little place is concerned, I don't mind so much. He should be pleased that we've come to him instead of going somewhere more expensive.'

'Yes, that will be nice.'

'Now, you'll laugh at me, but I've just thought of a dish I've always wanted to eat. I've never heard of it and it will be very expensive. You could do it here as well as anywhere, but it would mean too much waste. What I want is a concoction made up entirely of chicken oysters. For the two of us you'd probably need about twenty chickens, so we couldn't possibly do it at home. But at a big restaurant, where they can use the rest of the chickens, they can produce it. Now will you consider how you would do it yourself? Don't tell me. And then we'll order it at some restaurant a day or two in advance. I'm afraid we'll have to go to a big place for that. The little man we're going to on Friday couldn't cope with an extra twenty chickens.'

'All right. We'll do that next week.'

'What a glutton I am,' said Douglas. 'D'you know that so far we've only talked about ourselves and our very petty little luxuries.'

'I agree with you about everything,' said Sheila, 'except about my hair. That is not a petty little luxury but one of the most important things in my life after you and the children.'

'All right,' said Douglas. 'You shall have your hair. Now we'd better start making a list of the people we're going to send cheques to. Let's deal with people first and institutions afterwards. But perhaps first of all we'd better decide on how much we'd want to keep for ourselves. What d'you say to £100,000.'

'We don't need anything like that,' said Sheila.

'You don't know what you're talking about. At the present rate of inflation the capital value, whatever we do with it, will be reduced considerably every year, and we shall be liable to all sorts of taxes. We shall need a large income to be able to pay school and university fees and so on without having to worry how we're going to go on living. And then if one of us dies—'

'Don't speak of it,' said Sheila.

'We must. We've got to be sensible about it. But we'll need expert advice as to what we're to do with the money for ourselves. All I say now is that we shouldn't give away more than four hundred thousand. I suppose we shall have to pay transfer tax on that. Then we'll have to insure our lives so that the children don't have to pay what's left in tax if we're both killed in a car accident. And it won't take long to give away four hundred thousand pounds. I mean, if we give fifty thousand pounds for cancer research, it's only a drop in the ocean to them. I tell you one thing I'd like to do. I'd like to give ten thousand pounds to the Freewheelers.'

'Who are they?'

'Don't you remember? They were mentioned on Nationwide. Young men on motor bicycles who are available day and night to get blood or drugs or whatever in the case of emergency. It's a wonderful idea. It gives them something exciting to do and does a lot of good in the process. They're given a little blue light on the motor cycle so that they can feel they're almost policemen. They get a great kick out of it. A lot of these young men who behave anti-socially today only do so because they're not directed in the right way. This has been a very violent century and many people who are alive today have experienced two world wars so it's in the blood of normal young people to want some form of excitement, whether its running riot at football matches or on trains or along the High Street of the nearest town, it doesn't very much matter to them. And I bet you many of them would be absolutely satisfied with this sort of work. They've got first-class fast motor bikes and really feel they're important while they're doing the job. And so they are. I saw on TV some months ago that they were going to have to close down because the motor cycle company could no longer afford to supply them with new bicycles each year. So that's one thing I'd like to support and see extended.'

'I wonder if there are any ex-Borstal boys among them? It's worth finding out, if we're going to support it. I'll get in touch with the Home Office about it. That really is a bright idea of yours. It's one thing to go to the Home Office and say you think this ought to be done or that ought to be done or why don't you start up a scheme for this or the other. They're used to that sort of thing and, although they take notice of these schemes when they're not too mad, there's not much they can do about them. But if we can go to them and say we're prepared to finance a scheme, that's a horse of a very different colour.'

'As a matter of fact,' said Douglas, 'it would be quite a good idea to do it through one of the media, probably television. They know how to approach subjects like this and to put the right pressure on Government departments. They'd be in a very strong position if we were prepared to back it with real money. But the sad thing is that half a million is nothing like enough. There are so many things we'd like to do.'

'So you think we'd better win another five hundred thousand pounds?'

'We could use every penny of it,' said Douglas, 'and a good deal more. The Government has nothing like enough money to do all sorts of things that I'm sure that politicians of every party would like to see done. Now, if we had a few million pounds we could do quite a bit. So I'm afraid we'll have to lower our sights and try to do things we really can do. But the Freewheelers really will be something. And if we can bring your Borstal boys into it so much the better. And young criminals as well. I'm sure that some of them go in for crime for the excitement.'

'If you're not careful,' said Sheila, 'before we've finished we shall be having an overdraft. I'm all in favour of helping everybody we possibly can and for using the money to the best possible advantage. That will be the great fun of it. But we've got to see that neither we nor our children are ever short again.'

'You can never be sure of that. There could be a wealth tax which took it all away in one fell swoop. And that would be the end of the pools. And premium bonds. No, I don't think they'll do that just yet. And let me remind you that it was you who said that £100,000 was more than we needed for ourselves. I quite agree with you that we've got to be selfish for ourselves and our children. But fortunately there isn't a great deal that we want and, if we do buy a country cottage in Wales or

Scotland or somewhere, it will still retain its value to some extent, whatever we pay for it.'

'That's one advantage of all this publicity,' said Sheila. 'We shan't be tempted to go and live elsewhere and give up our friends here because, wherever we went, people would know who we were.'

'I suppose that once we've got through the first few months,' said Douglas, 'we shall live it down in a way. After all I shall go on being a librarian and you'll go on cooking my food. We shall live in much the same way as we have done in the past, except that we shall be able to afford the higher standard which we both like.'

'No more British sherry,' said Sheila.

'It's a pity they can't make sherry in England but they can't and except in a few exceptional vineyards, like Hambledon, they can't make wine either. Those terrible home brewed clarets and burgundies would make me as sick as Henry was with the champagne. But there's something else I hadn't thought of which is far more serious than anything we've mentioned. I'm going to ring up Vulgans again and see if they'll call off the publicity.'

'Why? What is it?'

'Everybody will soon know that we're worth half a million. Aren't we putting the two girls at risk? Come to think of it, we're at risk too. I go off to work and the next thing I know is that you've been kidnapped. Or one of the girls is kidnapped from school. These things happen far too often. I'll put it to the Company that it isn't fair to put us at risk like that. Surely they'll be able to see it. And the encouragement that's given to kidnappers and blackmailers these days!'

Douglas telephoned Vulgans' Pools and asked to speak to a director. When he said who he was, he had little difficulty in being put through.

'What can I do for you, Mr Barton?'

'It's the publicity I'm worried about.'

'But surely you've had all that out with our representative already?'

'Yes, I know,' said Douglas, 'but I didn't mention to him a very important point which, curiously enough, has only just occurred to me. When all the papers and television people come out with our name and faces and so forth people will know, for example, that we have two daughters aged fifteen still at school. My wife and I are extremely worried that attempts might be made to kidnap one of them. Or both for that matter. There's so much of this happening all over the world. Do you think it's fair to let us take this risk?'

'Shouldn't you have thought of that before when you failed to put a cross in the box?

'Of course. And I must say my wife thought it had been put in. That was our mistake, I grant you. Now I quite follow that publicity is very important to you, but isn't the liberty and possibly the life of our family more important than that?'

'Mr Barton,' said the director, 'there are still a large number of people in this country who have very substantial means. And their safety, and the safety of their families, is certainly at risk these days. You will simply be one more. Why should the kidnappers pay their attention to you any more than they do to a pop star or a film star or a politician? What about the members of the Cabinet? Are not their wives and daughters permanently at risk? I expect some of them get police protection. They can't all get it for twenty-four hours every day, you know, but, if you're worried about this, I'll you what you can do. There are two things. First of all you can probably get the police to put an alarm bell in your house in every room and, if you press it, it will ring in the police station and help will come along as quickly as possible. Secondly, you're going to be worth half a million pounds and, if you're worried about the safety of your daughters or your wife or indeed of yourself, you could spend some of it on getting protection from a security firm. That will be expensive but you can easily afford it. If, for

example, you have your daughters under twenty-four hour surveillance for, say, three months, that might cost you £500 a
week, six or seven thousand pounds. If you wanted to, you
could spend another six or seven thousand pounds, or possibly
a little less, on having your wife under surveillance. She won't
like it, but, if it will make you happier while you're at work,
it's probably a good idea. By the end of three months you should
be in no worse a position than all the rest of the rich people in
the country. And, if I may say so, it will then be more likely
that you will be run over or have an accident in your car than
that any of your family will be kidnapped. After all, the
number of kidnappings in this country in the last two years
has been very small indeed. I grant you that we live in a lawless
age and it may go up. But doesn't my suggestion answer your
problem?'

'It's certainly a help,' said Douglas, 'and I'm very much
obliged to you. Of course I don't mind the money in the least.
But haven't I read that you get crooks in security firms as well?'

'That's quite true but there are very few and I'm quite sure
that they take every care to see that they employ only people
of integrity. There are a few black sheep – there are in the
police – but you emphasise your fears to the firm that you
employ and try to make sure that they will take great care to
see that the people they send to you are of proved integrity.
As you probably realise, we are concerned with security in this
firm. We have to be. So I know a good deal about it.'

'Then I can't persuade you,' asked Douglas, 'to cry off the
publicity?'

'I'm afraid not. But I can assure you that we'll make that as
pleasant as possible and I hope that you and your family will
eventually enjoy it. And I'm sure it will make you happier if
you adopt the course which I've suggested. Would you like me
to recommend a security firm or d'you prefer to make your
own enquiries?'

'I'd be very grateful for your recommendation.'

'I suggest one of the smaller firms. I'm not criticising the bigger firms in the least, but there's one small firm I know which is particularly careful in its selection of employees. They call themselves Round the Clock Limited.'

'Thank you very much,' said Douglas, and the conversation ended. He told Sheila what the director had suggested. 'There's no time to be lost. When I go up to town tomorrow I'll go and see these Round the Clock people and arrange to have a twenty-four hour guard on the girls and on you.'

'Why me? I should hate it.'

'I'm sure you would but I shouldn't have a minute's peace, unless I thought you were protected. Look at the number of ways in which you could be kidnapped. A pretended accident on the road. If you saw a person lying in the road you'd have to get out of the car. Or two young men could force themselves into the house while you were alone. It may cost us as much as £20,000 in three months but we shan't notice it.'

'Perhaps you're right,' said Sheila. 'But I hope it won't look too obvious.'

'I'd better try and arrange to take a fortnight's holiday. With all that's going to happen to us in the next few weeks, I shall need it.'

'When are you going to tell Edward?' asked Sheila.

'I've told Theo to tell him now. There's no point in waiting. It's much better to tell him ourselves than for him to read it in the press or see it on television. If he's a success with Theo, he'll be able to put up his wages.'

'What about Henry and Mrs Mountjoy?'

'You're quite right. It will be better to tell them too. They might feel hurt if they didn't know in advance. I'll tell you another thing we're going to have to do. We're going to get thousands of letters and we'll get people calling at the house as well. We must have an efficient secretary to help us to deal with them. I'll make that the second thing I'll do in town after I've dealt with security.'

'Are you beginning to wish it hadn't happened?'

'Good gracious, no. It's a godsend. But I am rather appalled at the thought of what it's going to mean. But we can't have it both ways. We're going to have to go through an awful lot that we don't like in the next month or so and in return for that we'll be able to pay the school fees without wondering whether we shall have enough left in the account to pay the rates as well. It's curious, though, that getting security in one way makes us vulnerable in another. It wasn't the case twenty-five years ago. The trouble is that people all over the world are giving into these kidnappers.'

'Wouldn't you if one of the girls were involved?'

'Of course I would. But in fact it would be wrong to do so. It would mean that other girls and other children in the future would be even more at risk. If criminals knew for certain that they'd get nothing out of kidnapping except prison if they were caught, they wouldn't go in for it. One of these days the Government will have to make a firm stand. At the present moment nearly every country yields to political kidnappings and this encourages other people to follow suit. And so it will go on. But I grant you that it's easy enough to say this when one's own family isn't involved. If I were Home Secretary and you were kidnapped I'd prefer to release all the prisoners in gaol in order to get you back if I could. It's quite true that, when I say they'll have to make a stand, I mean that the other man will have to make a stand. Now what about a secretary? She'll have to live in.'

'Then I'd better choose her,' said Sheila.

'You can vet her,' said Douglas. 'But I'd better find one when I go up to town and see the security people. We shall need someone at once.'

The next day Douglas arranged with Round the Clock Limited to keep a twenty-four hour surveillance on both girls and on Sheila. He then went to a large secretarial agency.

'We want a really intelligent young woman,' he said. 'Preferably a widow with no children. It will be quite an interesting job. My wife has just won a large football pool and we shall want a lot of help. In consequence the hours will be irregular and we want someone who can live in. It's only a temporary job and will probably last say about three months. I'm prepared to pay well for the right person, but she must be educated, sensible and not frightened of work.'

'As a matter of fact,' said the manageress, 'I've someone in the next room who's just come to interview me. She might be the person you need. How much would you be prepared to pay?'

'Within reason,' said Douglas, 'whatever she wants. The important thing from our point of view is to get the right person and she must of course be of unquestionable integrity.'

'I'll introduce you to her,' said the manageress. 'Could you come this way, please?' She led Douglas into another room where an attractive young woman was sitting.

'This is Mrs Hillyard,' said the manageress. 'Mr Barton is looking for someone for a special job which will last about three months. He'll explain it to you himself. I'll leave you to talk it over.'

Douglas was very pleased with what he saw. The fact that he was a faithful husband did not blind him in any way to other women's charms. For a moment he wondered what Sheila's reaction would be if Mrs Hillyard came to stay with them. For a split second he also wondered what his own reaction would be if he saw a lot of Mrs Hillyard.

'I've recently lost my husband,' she said, 'and want to get down to work as soon as possible. I was married for three years and before that I was a trained secretary and held down some important positions. I was for five years with some well-known publishers as secretary to the managing director.'

'Who were they?'

'Greenby & Medlicott.'

'They're a very big firm,' said Douglas. 'And before that?'

'Before that I was in industry for a couple of years. I left because I didn't much care for it. I liked the people but the work didn't really suit me. Might I ask what the position would be with you?'

Douglas explained. 'So you can see that I don't really know exactly what there will be to do. I only know that there will be a lot. We shall get a vast number of begging letters and probably a fair number of beggars. My wife and I want to help people. That's the best part of having a win like this. But I expect that very few people who write begging letters purely for themselves are worth helping. Though the odd one may be.'

'It sounds quite interesting,' said Mrs Hillyard.

'Then there will be people to deal with personally. I'm sure some people will come to the house. I don't want them to be turned away automatically. But you always have to consider the security aspect. One of the things we actually worry about is the possible kidnapping of our daughters. Or of my wife or even me. Someone might come along in the guise of a beggar to case the joint. We want to be particularly on the look-out for that, so that we can get on to the police at once. I'll explain to you the security arrangements which I have already made. In other words we want somebody to be with us the whole of the time, to protect us from unwanted callers and to help us generally in the very difficult few weeks or months which we're going to have once the news becomes public. It's all because we forgot to put the X in the right place and the pools company quite naturally want all the publicity it can get and I've had to agree to it. I tried to persuade them otherwise but it was no good. First of all, do you like the idea of the job?'

'Very much,' said Mrs Hillyard. 'It sounds quite exciting.'

'It might be too exciting,' said Douglas, 'and that's one of the reasons I want a really efficient secretary. Now, if you'd like the job, d'you mind telling me something about yourself? How were you educated?'

'I went to St Enoch's at Oxford where I got a degree in English.'

'That's fine. As a matter of fact, I'm the librarian of the New Fiction Library.'

'That is most interesting.'

'Forgive my asking this but I assume you can give references as to character.'

'Certainly. I have two written references with me and you can ring up the people concerned and ask for confirmation.'

'Now, about salary. As you will realise in this job there will be no particular hours. We might want your help in the middle of the night. Time off and all that sort of thing will have to be arranged as we go along. Accordingly, naturally we expect to pay a good salary. Would fifty or sixty pounds a week suit you?'

'I think it would be very fair,' said Mrs Hillyard. 'Can you give me any idea of how long it will be for? You said some weeks or three months or something like that, but I should like to know how long I'm secure for.'

'That's fair enough,' said Douglas. I'll undertake to make it not less than three months, but, if we find things are tailing off at the end of two months, there will be no objection to your applying for something else.'

'That will suit me very well.' Mrs Hillyard looked in her bag and produced two references. 'Perhaps you'd like to ring up from here to confirm them? I'll go out of the room while you do.'

'Before you do that,' said Douglas, 'I suppose I ought to have some sort of proof of your identity.'

'You mean,' said Mrs Hillyard, 'that everything I've said might be true of someone else?'

'I'm sure you'll understand,' said Douglas, 'that we can't take any chance.'

'Of course. I quite understand. I've a driving licence and a bank card. Will they do? I could give you a specimen signature as well.'

'It's very good of you to be so understanding,' said Douglas. 'It would be very embarrassing otherwise.'

As a result of this interview and of two telephone calls to the referees, Douglas, having consulted Sheila, arranged with Susan Hillyard to come down and take up residence the next day.

By the time Douglas got home a lot had happened. Vulgans Pools had finally confirmed that there was no other winner and that Sheila would get half a million pounds. They had also arranged that the presentation would be made in a private room at the Savoy at lunch time on Wednesday afternoon. Sheila and Douglas and Theo were to be interviewed on television the same evening.

Susan Hillyard arrived on Tuesday evening. Sheila swallowed slightly when she saw how attractive she was but she liked the look of her and, as Susan was a very friendly person, they got along very well from the start.

Douglas and Sheila decided to break the news to Henry and Mrs Mountjoy and Edward at the same time. So Theo brought Edward in at drinks time and Henry brought in Mrs Mountjoy. Edward was obvious much taken with Susan and stationed himself as near to her as he could. After Douglas had told them what it was all about, Henry congratulated them.

'No more British sherry,' he said. 'But by jove I'm going to have some competition. Everybody will be trying to scrounge from you now.'

'You've got quite a good lead, if I may say so,' said Douglas.

'Up to the moment,' said Henry, 'true enough, but if you'll forgive my saying so, up to now there's been hardly anything worth scrounging. Now the sky's the limit.'

'I feel quite sure,' said Mrs Mountjoy, 'that the prize could not be in better hands than those of Mr and Mrs Barton and, if Mr Bunting wants to keep me as his housekeeper, he will treat you no differently now that you've won this big prize than he has in the past.'

'I promise that,' said Henry. 'But the stakes will just be a bit higher.'

'I suppose you realise,' said Edward, 'that you will now be first priority for all the crooks in England.'

'We've thought of that,' said Douglas, 'and I think I've taken all the precautions I properly can.'

'You mean as far as violence is concerned?'

'Yes.'

'When it comes to fraud I might be able to help you.'

'Are you a lawyer then?' asked Susan.

'No, though I've learned quite a lot of law in my time. No, up till now I've been on the wrong side of the law.'

'D'you mean you've actually been to prison?' said Susan in a way which showed that she appeared to be rather appalled at the information.

'I'm afraid so,' said Edward, 'but I've turned over a new leaf. And you'll have the advantage of having an expert on your side, apart from the fact that I may know some of the people who try to muscle in on you. I ought also to be able to spot the handiwork of a good many of the people I don't know.'

'You should be able to help me then,' said Susan. 'I've got to look through the post first.'

'Don't hesitate to come to me,' said Edward. 'I shall only be at the bottom of the garden and I'm sure my employer will let me off for a few minutes to come and help you.'

'Certainly,' said Theo. 'We're all in this together and we shall need all the help we can possibly get.'

'Don't hesitate to call on us,' said Henry. 'We've a couple of spare bedrooms. Where is Mrs Hillyard staying, by the way?'

'With us, thank you,' said Douglas.

'We've an extra bathroom too,' said Henry.

'Thank you, Henry,' said Sheila, 'but we can manage all right. It is very kind of you.'

After Henry and Mrs Mountjoy and Edward had left, Douglas apologised to Susan for not having told her about Edward before she came.

'I felt awkward about doing it,' he said. 'I hoped he would tell you himself but I didn't ask him to do so. But I'm beginning to believe that he really wants to lead a normal, honest life and it seemed to me to be a bit unfair to him to tell you what he'd been. I suppose,' he added, 'I ought to add that consciously or unconsciously I thought you might refuse to come.'

'I wouldn't have,' said Susan, 'as a matter of fact. It makes the job even more interesting. I like meeting people. People of every kind. Good, bad and indifferent. Though from my experience there's often as much good in the bad as there is bad in the good. What do we mean by good anyway?'

'If you meet our Aunt Agatha, who is most appropriately named,' said Douglas, 'you will certainly know what I mean by good. But she's a very exceptional person. She's never yet been able to see any bad in anyone but she's not sentimental or mawkish, and she's very understanding of the modern generation. She would never dream of using bad language herself, but if ever by accident – and I assure you it would be by accident – I let out a four-letter word in front of her, the most she would do would be to ask what it actually meant. She always tries to see the best in everything and everybody. That doesn't mean to say that she doesn't realise what's going on all around her. She's a very intelligent woman. Apart from that, she paints the most beautiful water colours. I say, let's ring her up and tell her now. She's awfully good on the phone and she loves a chat on it.'

'Good idea,' said Sheila.

Five minutes later Aunt Agatha was answering the phone.

'Agatha Crosthwaite speaking.'

'It's Douglas here. How are you?'

'Very well, my dear, thank you. No bad news, I hope.'

'Oh no.'

'Is Theo going to get married then?'

'Not as far as we know.'

'Then you're suddenly coming up to see me?' She spoke in a loud voice which could be heard by Sheila as well.

She shouted: 'We shall be coming soon, I hope.'

'Then that isn't why you're ringing?'

'No, it isn't.'

'Don't tell me. Let me think. I know. You've won £75,000 on a premium bond and you're going to take me round the world.'

'You're pretty warm. Would you like to go round the world?'

'Not unless you would. Two or three times round my garden's good enough for me. Then I'm afraid Sheila must have won a football pool.'

'Guilty,' said Douglas.

'You know I don't really approve of gambling, but it's a very mild form and I approve of Sheila. Why are you ringing me up?'

'There isn't much fun in winning something like this unless we all share it. We wondered what you'd like.'

'That's very sweet. How much have you won?'

'Half a million pounds.'

'Heavens! Are you serious, Douglas?'

'I am.'

'Good gracious. I'll make a list. It's a very pleasant thought. Think of the books you'll be able to give me. It's so tantalising when you read a review and you want the book and you can't afford to buy it when it's four or five pounds at least. I'll send you a list at once. Then, what else is there? I know. I shall go in for orchids. Outside and in. You can build me a greenhouse. Now what else can I think of? I know. You did say half a million?'

'Yes,' said Douglas.

'Well, we want a new village hall and we've had an estimate

for six thousand pounds. Make it ten and we shall be able to have a better one. Then, if we got a really good organ for the church, we might be able to get a first-class organist and a few singers for the choir. Shall I go on?'

'Are you sure the local council doesn't want a new town hall?' said Douglas.

'In my view it should,' said Aunt Agatha. 'But the present one is perfectly serviceable and I don't want to waste my money on that. Oh yes, there's another thing. I think we should start a motor car service to take the old people from the Home to a theatre every now and then. I should think if you invested ten or fifteen thousand pounds that would produce enough to give it a start. Perhaps that's enough to begin with. I'll put the others down on a list.'

'Would you mind putting down the ones you've mentioned as well?'

'Oh certainly, I won't let you forget those. But how nice of you to give me this chance. What did I say about gambling? I withdraw every word. D'you know, Douglas, this is a wonderful moment in my life. How much may I spend? Would a hundred thousand pounds be too much?'

'That's without the books, I take it?' said Douglas.

'Oh, of course. They'll be a gift from you.'

'Would you mind making it fifty thousand to begin with, Aunt Agatha. You see we're going to have an awful lot of things we'd like to do and we haven't really started to sort things out at all yet.'

'Of course, dear. It was greedy of me. No. Fifty thousand pounds will do very nicely. When may I expect the cheque? You see, I don't want to raise people's hopes until I've actually got the money.'

'But we haven't actually got it yet.'

'Oh dear. Is there any doubt about it?'

'No. We're getting it tomorrow.'

'Well then, if you send it to me by first-class post I shall get it on Thursday. But then I suppose you want to get the cheque cleared first. Have it specially cleared. Then it will be credited to your account by Thursday and you can send me my cheque on the same day and I'll get it on Friday. How will that be?'

'Yes. I think we'll be able to do that.'

'That will be wonderful. I'll go and see my bank manager tomorrow. I'll put the whole lot on deposit to begin with. I'm sure that's the safest thing to do. Everything's so chancey now. Three years ago I'd have bought blue chips but not today, thank you.'

'Unless,' said Douglas, 'Sheila's success has encouraged you to have a little flutter.'

'That's a very fair dig. No, I shall have mine where I can see it – on deposit. That should bring in four or five thousand a year anyway. Is Sheila there? I'd like to have a word with her.'

'Yes, of course.'

Sheila came to the telephone. 'Hullo, Aunt Agatha.'

'Hullo, my darling. You're a very clever girl. How happy you've made me. I'm going to have the time of my life. How very selfish of me. What are you going to do with it? I mean with the balance of four hundred and fifty thousand.'

'We don't really know yet, Aunt Agatha. We shall give a lot of it away.'

'Now be very careful about that. Once people know you've got it they'll all be clamouring round you like hungry wolves. Of course some of them will be hungry. It will be difficult to tell the hungry from the greedy. If you treat everyone like you've treated me, you'll have nothing left for yourselves. So let me be a lesson to you. Now, tell me the truth. You didn't expect me to ask for anything, did you.'

'We never thought about it,' said Sheila. 'We just wanted you to know.'

'But I bet it's shaken Douglas. He's had to sit down. I tell you what. If you add another ten thousand I'll give you the little water colour you've always admired. The one in my dining room of the mill at Tapley No, I wasn't serious. But tell Douglas, if he does find that he's got any left over which he doesn't know what to do with, I'll find a little niche for it. Now, when are you coming to see me?'

Douglas put his hand over the mouthpiece and whispered to Sheila. 'Tell her we can't make any plans until we know what's going to happen, but we hope in three or four weeks' time.' Sheila repeated this to the old lady.

'I quite understand. It will be lovely to see you, whenever you do come. Meantime you can think of me having fun with your fifty thousand pounds. Douglas did say I could have it by Friday, didn't he?' And the old lady rang off.

'Have you any other aunts?' asked Susan.

'Not like Aunt Agatha,' said Douglas, 'fortunately. But she's quite right, you know. She'll make very good use of that fifty thousand.'

'I daresay,' said Sheila, 'but we've got to think this out very carefully.'

'That's what we've got Susan for,' said Douglas. 'Our first priority is safety. The second is getting through the next three weeks and the third will be the distribution. Susan must get from us all the individuals and institutions we'd like to benefit and then she can add any suggestions of her own and all the time she must bear in mind that we've got to have enough to live on ourselves and to provide for the future of the children. Now, Susan, I've given you the names of our solicitors and accountant. Don't bother about them at the moment, but, when you've dealt with the other two priorities and we've given you all the names we can think of, it will be your job to present us with a suggested distribution list.'

'That will be fun,' said Susan. 'You did say I might make any suggestions of my own?'

'Certainly.'

'I've a passion for lifeboatmen,' said Susan. 'When people sail across the Atlantic for their own benefit they make a fortune and get knighted. The lifeboatmen are on call every day of every year and save people from drowning and get nothing at all for it, except the thanks of the people they save and their relatives. Sometimes the relatives may not even thank them. The lifeboatmen do it because they've got a vocation that way and not in the hope of reward, but I think that far too much fuss is made of people who are very courageous and endure fantastic danger but who do it almost entirely for their own benefit. And far too little fuss is made of people who are risking their lives daily, like firemen and lifeboatmen.'

'I quite agree,' said Douglas. 'And I'm sure Sheila does too.' Sheila nodded. 'So you can certainly put them down.'

'I hope you'll let me see Aunt Agatha sometime,' said Susan. 'She must be a wonderful old lady. I can see her sitting down now with a pencil and paper, working out the interest on fifty thousand pounds and how she's going to spend the capital and the interest. I'll tell you something. If you're not careful she'll be asking for that other fifty thousand pounds too. She's obviously got quite big ideas and, if you've got big ideas, you could very easily run through several million, let alone fifty or a hundred thousand.'

'It's a pity we've let her have so much to begin with,' said Douglas.

'Couldn't help it,' said Sheila. 'Don't forget she asked for double. I wouldn't have had the nerve to halve it.'

CHAPTER NINE

Vision On

For those pools winners who want not only the money but the publicity as well, the day on which they receive the cheque must be a great day indeed. But the Bartons, though still delighted that their financial worries were at an end, woke up on the morning when they were to receive the cheque full of apprehension. They were not people who wanted publicity in any way. They had never asked for it and it had never appeared likely that it would be thrust upon them. Although it was the consequences of the publicity that they feared most, they hated the idea of the method by which they were going to receive it. They had agreed to do as Vulgans Pools wanted, because they realised that, if they resisted publicity, they would get it anyway and it would be much more unpleasant trying unsuccessfully to avoid it than, as Mr Reynolds had suggested, to go along with the pool promoters.

Dulcie Mainwaring, who was going to present them with the cheque, was quite a competent little actress who had made a name in a television series. It was called *The Maiden Aunt* and it was about an attractive woman of forty who remained an aunt and a maiden in spite of the overtures of twenty-six different kinds of men. There had been two series of thirteen episodes each and so far the ingenious authors of the series had managed to find twenty-six new ways in which the nubile aunt had evaded her pursuers. When suggestions were made towards the end of the second series that in the last episode the whole idea would end with Dulcie getting married, thousands of angry letters were sent in by viewers of every kind, so that the authors were persuaded to tax their ingenuity even more and to produce another thirteen episodes.

The first of these was due to be broadcast shortly after Dulcie's presentation of the cheque to Sheila. Until she was selected to play the maiden aunt, Dulcie's career in the theatre had been a very ordinary one and she was quite unknown to West End playgoers, even though occasionally they had had the opportunity of seeing her playing some small part. Unfortunately neither Sheila nor Douglas had looked at a single one of the series. They did not look at much on television except news and documentaries, though there had been two series which they had followed with much pleasure. But *The Maiden Aunt* was not one of them and from the reviews which they had read they were pretty certain that it was not for them.

'What shall I talk to her about?' said Douglas.

'I shouldn't worry about that,' said Sheila. 'When you're going to a drinks party you don't worry about what you're going to talk about. This girl won't be any different. If you ask me, if she's the talkative type she'll be like everybody else is going to be and be questioning us as to what we're going to do with the money.'

'That gives me an idea,' said Douglas. 'We could invent a few things, so long as we make it plain in the end that we're only pulling their legs. Let's think of a few societies we could form as – oh, I don't know – something like The Society for Taking the Gilt off the Gingerbread and then explain that the shiny part of the gingerbread was produced by using a substance to which I'll give some fanciful name which we consider is bad for people. Like the complaints we're getting against fluoride. I don't think that's a very good one but you see what I mean.

If one is serious enough about a subject, people will believe you. We might get Theo to suggest some inventions. If they're not too absurd, in the present state of technology people will accept the possibility.'

'Well,' said Sheila, 'you can do what you like, but I'm going to be my ordinary sweet self.'

'We shall want Susan with us,' said Douglas.

'Why particularly?' asked Sheila.

'Because she's got to be in on the whole thing. She must know exactly what happens.'

'Then you'd better tell them there'll be an extra one for lunch,' said Sheila.

Some three hours after this conversation Douglas, Sheila, Theo and Susan presented themselves at the Savoy Hotel where they were met by the representative of Vulgans Pools. It was not the man who had originally called on them but a very cheerful individual who was very much like several of the television compères rolled into one.

'Well, here we are,' he said. 'My name – God forgive my parents – is Lancelot Hermitage. Please call me Lance. You, I take it, are Douglas. And you are Sheila. This is one of your daughters and your son.'

'Our twin daughters are fifteen.'

'I knew that,' said Mr Hermitage, 'and I must confess that the sample you've brought is very well developed.'

'This is my secretary, Susan Hillyard, but you're right in thinking this is our son Theo.'

'Well, well, well. Why didn't you bring the girls? The headmistress didn't agree, I suppose? Thought it would be bad for them. Personally I think she's quite right, but it's a pity all the same. Are they pretty?'

'Not bad,' said Douglas.

'They'd have added a bit of colour.'

'Well,' said Douglas, 'you'll have to make do with what you've got, I'm afraid. And as Dulcie Mainwaring's one of the party

I don't think she'd be very pleased if you told her that it lacked colour.'

'And,' said Sheila, 'as Susan and I are two of the party, neither of us is very pleased at being told that.'

'Splendid, splendid,' said Mr Hermitage. 'I can see we're going to get on famously. Sometimes these gatherings are a bit stiff, you know, and I have to spend a lot of time in oiling the works. But I can see they're well oiled already. Not in the alcoholic sense. Not yet, that is, but I shall hope to remedy that in the next few minutes. If you'll now come with me to the Utopia Room, I'll introduce you to Miss Mainwaring. A very suitable room, don't you think, for today's ceremony, Utopia? By the way,' he said, as they went along the corridor, 'none of you, I hope, has a weak heart.'

'Have you, Susan?' asked Douglas.

'I don't think so.'

'Then none of us has.'

'Good. Because it was too much for one couple I brought here. I suppose I should have asked but I didn't. They both had weak hearts. Fortunately the Charing Cross Hospital isn't far away and we managed to keep it out of the Press, but it almost spoiled the brandy and cigars. Now, here we are. Come in.' He led them into the room called Utopia, where Dulcie Mainwaring was already seated drinking a champagne cocktail. 'Here we are then,' said Mr Hermitage. 'May I present Douglas and Sheila Barton, Theodore Barton and no relation, Susan Hillyard, to the maiden aunt in the person of Miss Dulcie Mainwaring.'

They exchanged greetings and sat down.

'It's very good of you to come to this ceremony,' said Douglas to Dulcie.

'I do get a fee, you know.'

'All the same, it's very good of you. I'd say the same thing to any actress who was playing a part in a play I'd written. I'd thank her very much for playing it, although I know that she'd be paid for the part and, indeed, in some cases her agents would be pressing her to accept it.'

'My agent didn't press for this,' said Dulcie. 'They came to him. What was your last play, may I ask?'

'Oh, I'm not a playwright,' said Douglas.

'What a pity.'

'I hadn't thought of that,' said Douglas, 'but I see what you mean. I'm sorry.'

'Ah, here are the photographers,' said Mr Hermitage. 'You're a bit late, aren't you?'

'This is the time we were told to be here,' said the elder of them.

'Never mind. You're here now. That's all that matters. Now, first of all, please, we'd like a picture of Miss Mainwaring giving the cheque to Mrs Barton. You set it as you think fit and I'll tell you if I agree.'

'Well,' said the photographer, 'I think everybody should have a glass of champagne in their hands. Miss Mainwaring can have her glass on the table, if she prefers not to have both her hands engaged.'

'Do you happen to be engaged?' asked Mr Hermitage.

'Certainly not,' said Dulcie. 'But d'you think I'd admit it if I were? It would be terribly bad for the series.'

The photographers arranged the scene as they wanted it and asked Mr Hermitage's approval.

'That seems very satisfactory,' he said, 'except for most of their faces. The only one who looks as though she's enjoying it is Miss Mainwaring.'

'I'll get a smile out of them before I take it,' said the senior photographer. But Douglas had difficulty in smiling. He was not an actor and his face, when it was in repose, was inclined to look as though he was thinking depressing thoughts.

'Now, Douglas,' said Mr Hermitage, 'that won't do at all. Look at your wife. She's got a proper sense of the occasion.' Douglas gave a watery grin.

'I think that's worse than the other,' said the senior photographer.

'I quite agree,' said Mr Hermitage. 'How you can look so glum with a half-million-pound cheque just about to be given to your wife by this lovely girl, who has so far been pursued by twenty-six men without success, absolutely beats me. Suppose you were the twenty-seventh. You wouldn't get very far with that face.'

'I'm very sorry,' said Douglas. 'I'm doing my best.'

'Presumably you do smile or laugh sometimes,' said Mr Hermitage. 'Shall I tell you a funny story?'

'All right,' said Douglas. 'Fire ahead.'

But Mr Hermitage couldn't think of a funny story, nor could anyone else. After ten minutes of futile attempts to get some form of happiness on to Douglas's face, the senior photographer said : 'I tell you what. You'd better bury your face in a glass of champagne, then no one will notice.'

'Won't it look as though I've jumped the gun a bit?' said Douglas. 'Everybody else posing for a photograph and me guzzling away.'

'That's a splendid idea,' said Mr Hermitage. 'We'll call the picture Mr Barton Couldn't Wait.' At that moment Douglas actually smiled.

'Quick,' said the senior photographer. But by the time they'd taken the photograph Douglas's face was as grim as ever.

'Let's try again,' said Mr Hermitage. 'Suppose you have a couple of drinks first.'

'As a matter of fact,' said Douglas, 'I hate champagne. Could I have something else?'

'Of course. So that's the trouble, is it? What would you like?'

'A dry Martini.' A large dry Martini was ordered and Douglas drank half of it.

'Now, how d'you feel?' Mr Hermitage asked him.

'I feel extremely well,' said Douglas, 'but I cannot smile to order. Have you ever tried?'

'Often. Look.' And Mr Hermitage gave a beaming grin.

'Then you're an actor. It makes all the difference if you're not self-conscious. I am.'

'Your wife's not an actress and she manages it.'

'All women are actresses,' said Douglas.

'D'you know the story of the dirty window?' suddenly asked Mr Hermitage.

'No,' said Douglas.

'Well, I won't tell you. You couldn't see through it. Don't interrupt. I haven't finished. Now, Mr Barton, d'you know the story of the window you couldn't see through?'

'No,' said Douglas.

'I won't tell you,' said Mr Hermitage, 'in the presence of these ladies. It's dirty.' And he laughed hugely, but Douglas did not. Eventually they compromised by making Douglas hold up the glass so that it almost obscured his face, and Miss Mainwaring held out the cheque which Sheila took in one of her hands and each of them held up a glass of champagne. The photograph was taken and the first part of the proceedings was over. There were no problems during lunch and conversation seldom flagged. When very occasionally there was silence, Mr Hermitage came in with something like : 'I don't know what everybody else is doing, but I'm enjoying myself. Here's to Mrs Barton who's made me such a happy man.'

At the end of the proceedings Douglas and Sheila agreed that, apart from the trouble about the photograph, things could have been very much worse. But they still had the ordeal of the television interview in the evening.

They arrived at the studio in plenty of time and were told by the producer that they would have an opportunity of seeing quite an interesting performance before theirs. The B.B.C. had had a happy but somewhat mischievous idea of letting Harry Carpenter introduce the contest between Professor Cromarty and Dr Erskine on the subject of Sydney Smith, the great preacher and writer. Both contestants had stated publicly that they were the only people who knew all there was to be known on the subject and each had said that the other was somewhat mistaken in his facts and abysmally wrong in some of his opinions. One might have expected the interview to be conducted by Robin Day or Michael Charlton or Robert Kee or Robert Robinson or some other literary commentator, but some imp had whispered into the ear of the Director of Features that Harry Carpenter, the man who had commented on more fights in the ring than anyone else, was the man for the job.

When Mr Carpenter introduced the contestants he obviously had to resist the temptation of saying 'in the blue corner we have Professor Cromarty and in the red corner Dr Erskine.' But he said something very like it and added : 'I think I can promise viewers a sparkling contest. Neither of the contestants has ever lost a fight – or perhaps I should say has ever admitted losing a fight – and, like Muhammed Ali, each of them has claimed more than once that he is the greatest. They have never appeared on television together before and I think I can promise that you're in for a treat. Now, Professor Cromarty, you have stated publicly that Dr Erskine did not know what he was talking about. Would you care to enlarge upon that statement?'

'Very much,' said the professor. 'The law says that comment cannot be fair unless it is based on facts truly stated. It is just the same in literary history as it is in libel actions. You cannot make worthwhile comments unless you make them about something which has happened. In other words, your quotations must be correct. Dr Erskine does not even bother to look up the original source before he launches into quotation. Here he is quoting from the review of a book on public schools. "There is," he writes, "a set of sleek, well-dressed people, well in with people in power, who assemble daily at Mr Hatchard's shop." The "sleek" is Dr Erskine's word, not Sydney Smith's, nor would Sydney Smith, whose writing is, if I may say so, a good deal more literate than that of Dr Erskine, have written two "peoples" so close together. The correct quotation is as follows : "There is a set of well-dressed, prosperous gentlemen, who assemble daily at Mr Hatchard's shop; – clean, civil personages, well in with people in power, – delighted with every existing institution – and almost with every existing circumstance : – and, every now and then, one of these personages writes a little book; – and the rest praise that little book – expecting to be praised, in their turn, for their own little books : – and of these little books, thus written by these clean, civil personages, so expecting to be praised, the pamphlet before us appears to be one."

Mr Carpenter turned from the blue to the red corner. 'Well, Dr Erskine, what do you say to that?'

'I say,' said the doctor, 'that it is typical of the way Professor Cromarty goes about his business. He is all the time looking for trifles. I have little doubt that, if I cared to adopt the same attitude, I could find a great number of unimportant mistakes in his work. But as I have proved in my book *The Real Professor Cromarty* I have found a number of important mistakes too. Upon those mistakes I have built an unanswerable case against him. All he can do in return is to make the sort of piffling point which he has made tonight, which is not worthy of a sixth form schoolboy. Or perhaps it is.'

'You're not going to stand for that, I take it, Professor Cromarty?' said Mr Carpenter.

'That is mere polemics, mere vulgar abuse,' said Professor Cromarty. 'But it is not at all unexpected and entirely worthy of the speaker.'

'Well,' said Mr Carpenter, 'I think that was a fairly good first round. I would say that honours were about even.'

Meantime Professor Cromarty was looking at the ceiling and Dr Erskine was looking at the floor. Each of them was fairly angry and in a condition of mind where he was likely to make false points which rolled off the tongue satisfactorily, rather than to advance sound argument.

'Now, Dr Erskine,' said Mr Carpenter, 'would you like to put a point to Professor Cromarty?'

'Professor Cromarty,' began Dr Erskine, 'Sir Edward Makepeace, in his authoritative book on the subject, said by implication that you were talking nonsense when you wrote that Sydney Smith's flair for well-informed and pungent criticism derived from his early schooldays. Do you still maintain that you were correct?'

'There is no one,' said Professor Cromarty, 'who knows so little about literary history as Sir Edward Makepeace.'

'I'm afraid I must come in here,' said Mr Carpenter. 'I claim to know less about literary history than Sir Edward Makepeace.'

'Thank you, Mr Carpenter,' said Dr Erskine. 'That calls attention splendidly to the sort of statement that Professor Cromarty is constantly making. He is the master, if I may say so, of the wild exaggeration.'

'More polemics,' said Professor Cromarty. 'I will ignore them. All I need say is that it was Sir Edward Makepeace who was talking nonsense. If you will look at Chapter Eight in my book on the Scottish Clerics you will see that I fully justify my statement.'

'I take it that you don't agree with that, Dr Erskine?' said Mr Carpenter.

'You must forgive me for quoting from my own work but in a review which I wrote on the Scottish Clerics I said this: "Professor Cromarty has no doubt looked up the Dictionary of National Biography – probably the concise edition – in order to obtain some of the information which appears in this book. But I suppose we should be grateful for that, for when he quotes from the D.N.B. – I may add without the normal courteous acknowledgement – at least what he writes is intelligible. But when he gets into the realm of metaphysics he is as unintelligible as some psychiatrists giving evidence in a criminal trial, who seek to show that the accused who said when he was arrested,

'It's a fair cop. I've done it,' was living in a fantasy world and thought that he was a sixteenth century Japanese emperor, prodding one of his wives in an effort to encourage her to get him his early morning cup of tea".'

'How do you get out of that one?' asked Mr Carpenter of Professor Cromarty.

'I was always told,' said the professor, 'that nought added to nought still equalled nought. So when Dr Erskine quotes from his own work, which is of little or no value, he adds, as usual, nothing to the argument. If I may adapt Shakespeare, he adds less strength to that which has too little.'

Dr Erskine did not wait to be asked if he had any reply to that. He went on immediately: 'Professor Cromarty is talking about polemics. If that isn't an *argumentum ad hominem,* I don't know what is. And if this contest is going to deteriorate into a battle of abuse, I can think of nouns and adjectives which could very satisfactorily be applied to Professor Cromarty.'

In his turn the professor did not wait to be asked if he wanted to reply. 'I freely acknowledge,' he said, 'that, when it comes to argument by abuse, Dr Erskine is a past master in the art. I will give him pride of place on that subject any day.'

'I'm sorry, gentlemen,' said Mr Carpenter, 'but I'm afraid we've taken up all the time allotted to us. Personally I feel very cheated that the argument stopped at this most interesting stage, but we have in the studio the winner of the latest football pool, who has today become richer by five hundred thousand pounds and I'm sure that our viewers, though not richer in pocket are richer in mind, from having had the benefit of seeing these two great masters of the English tongue in action together. Professor Cromarty, thank you. Dr Erskine, thank you.' Mr Carpenter just managed to restrain himself from stepping in and holding up each of their hands.

Douglas and Sheila and Theo had been watching the battle from another studio, but it was now their turn to be watched.

'The first question,' said the interviewer addressing Sheila, 'is one I always ask on these occasions for the viewers' benefit if not for my own. Did you adopt any particular system or did you fill in your entry quite by chance?'

'I didn't fill it in at all,' said Sheila. 'My son Theo did that.'

'Then I ask him the same question.'

'I had a very definite plan of campaign,' said Theo. 'A few weeks previously it had shown itself to be of some use, as I won a very small prize. I think it was two pounds.'

'And what was your system?'

'I studied the form of the teams and I studied the advice given by a well-known tipster. I chose twenty-five matches where I thought there would be a good chance of a draw and then I crossed out all those matches which had been recommended by the tipster. In fact, I didn't cancel out enough. So I used another tipster until I'd only ten matches left. Then I entered the necessary crosses in a column of eight out of ten full permutations. My mother paid 22½p.'

'Now you've made it public,' said the interviewer, 'viewers may choose to adopt the same method. In fact the tipster whom you mainly used can claim credit for your success. It's just as useful to be told what matches to put in, if you're going to do the opposite, as it is if you're going to follow his advice.'

'I'm most grateful to him,' said Theo. 'Or my mother is.'

'And how did you all feel when you knew you'd won?'

'None of us believed it at first,' said Douglas. 'And then we wondered if the coupon had been received by the pools company. It was Theo who posted it and he's most reliable in the normal way but everyone can make mistakes. As a matter of fact, although he did post it, he did make one mistake.'

'What was that?'

'He forgot to put the cross in the no publicity box.'

'And that's why you're here tonight?'

'Entirely.'

'I believe that your job is that of librarian?'

'Quite true.'

'And, if you could have avoided all this publicity, you would have done so? I hope you're not hating this interview too much?'

'You're certainly making it as pleasant as possible, if I may say so, but we're not used to our pictures appearing in the paper or being asked questions in public, except occasionally by representatives of pollster firms.'

'Have you any idea what you're going to do with all your money?'

'We've some idea,' said Douglas, 'but we've got to think a good deal about it. But we're certainly going to help the Freewheelers to whom Nationwide gave some publicity a few months ago. We think it a very good idea to give these young men fast motor bikes to use for such good purpose.'

'I take it,' said the interviewer, 'that you're not going to blue it in riotous living. I'm afraid a very few successful competitors have done that.'

'I'm very sorry for them,' said Douglas. 'We're lucky in a way and unlucky in another way.'

'How d'you mean?'

'Some people don't know what to do with the money except to buy cars and houses and to lead a gay life. Our difficulty is that there is so much we want to do with the money that it's going to be very difficult leaving things out. I've mentioned the Freewheelers because they just happen to come into my head and because the B.B.C. is entitled to the credit for having made them known to us. But there are lots of other causes which deserve support. So many, in fact, that half a million pounds is nothing like enough to go round.'

'And that,' said the interviewer, 'is before looking after yourselves?'

'Oh no,' said Douglas. 'We shall look after ourselves within reasonable limits. It will be of very great help to us to have the extra money for the education of the two younger children and our own future prospects for retirement and so on. We shan't have to worry whether we can take a holiday in the future. I don't mind telling you that in common with many other middle-class people inflation has been affecting our standard of living very considerably. But for this windfall it would have gone on doing so to a considerable extent. But whatever the difficulties and inconveniences, which I agree are nothing like as much as many other people in the country experience, with all those difficulties we have always been very happy and we always shall be.'

'I take it you agree with that, Mrs Barton?'

'Entirely.'

'How would you describe a happy marriage?'

'For one thing I always look forward to seeing my husband come home in the evening.'

'And to his going off in the morning?' asked the interviewer.

'Yes, that too. It's nice to have the house to one's self sometimes.'

'How will you manage when he retires?'

'We'll still be very happy, but I'll have to adjust myself to the new position. For one thing I shall have to give him lunch every day. But retirement will have great advantages too. No doubt our children will be married by then and we shall be able to go to see them more than we could if Douglas were still at work.'

'Do you never quarrel?'

'I don't think so. Naturally we don't always agree. But you can disagree without quarrelling. I suppose in the earlier days of our marriage we had an argument or two but it's such a waste of energy. I think on the rare occasions when it happened we both found that and we soon got into the habit of always giving way to each other unless we felt very strongly on the point.'

'Suppose you both felt very strongly on a point?'

'Then usually Douglas gave way. Because of course he saw that I was right.'

133

'I would have said it was the other way round,' said Douglas. 'Sheila's a very intelligent woman and she soon realised that she was wrong and gave way gracefully.'

'And what about you?' said the interviewer, addressing Theo. 'How is it going to affect your life?'

'Not a great deal, but the important thing is that I shall know that Dad and Mum have not got to worry about where the next pound is coming from.'

'You speak as though they've had a hard time.'

'Of course not compared with people who haven't got enough to eat or haven't got a roof over their heads, but they have been awfully good to us children and I know that at the present moment they're finding it extremely difficult to carry on as they have done. Their standard of living has certainly dropped.'

'I believe that you've got a business of your own?'

'That's right.'

'Will you be extending that?'

'Only as I have done in the past. A little extra capital would be useful, but one of the dangers of a growing one-man business is that you may overreach yourself and I'm determined not to do that.'

'I believe you're a bit of an inventor.'

'That's right.'

'Can you tell us about anything you've invented recently?'

'No, I'm afraid not. At the moment it's confidential.'

'Is it something we shall see in the shops?'

'I rather doubt it.'

'From the way you've spoken up till now, Mr Barton, it doesn't sound as though you're going to change your house or your car.'

'Not our house certainly. But equally certainly we shall change our car. It's seven years old and starting to play up.'

'Any idea what you'll be getting?'

'We don't know yet. Nothing very spectacular. No Rolls-Royces, if that's what you mean.'

'It certainly looks as though you're going to make very good use of your winnings and that they're unlikely to do you any harm.'

'We hope not,' said Douglas. 'But who's to say for certain? If my wife hadn't won this pool we shouldn't have come here tonight and, when we go away from here, we may all be knocked down by a lorry.'

'But equally,' said the interviewer, 'if you hadn't won the pool and if you hadn't come here, you might all have gone to the theatre and been knocked down by a lorry on the way home.'

'You're quite right,' said Douglas. 'It isn't really very valuable to speculate on what would or would not have happened if one hadn't been late for a train.'

'Well, we'll send you home in a car and tell the driver to be very careful. Thank you very much, Mr and Mrs Barton, and Mr Barton junior.'

The interview ended and Douglas, Sheila and Theo were taken along to another room where Professor Cromarty and Dr Erskine were having drinks, but not together. Dr Erskine approached them.

'That was a very interesting interview, if I may say so,' he said, 'and very galling to me personally. I've just written a book which, according to one well-known reviewer, ought to sell a good many copies. I shall have to send a large proportion of the royalties which I shall get to the Inland Revenue. The book took me three years to write. However much trouble your son may have taken over filling in the football pool coupon, it can't have taken him more than a few hours at the most, and now your family is receiving half a million pounds. Do you call that justice?'

'No,' said Douglas. 'It isn't. But there are worse injustices than that, if *I* may say so.'

'Such as?'

'Well, the simplest one is if an innocent man is convicted of a crime. It's an unjust world, professor, and in human affairs there will always be injustice. You complain about having to pay tax on your royalties when you spent three years in writing the book. What about another man who spends a good number of years writing a book and gets no royalties because his publishers go bust? Or someone who writes a brilliant book which nobody publishes until after he's dead? And what about the injustices on the road when good and bad are killed alike?'

'You've made your point, thank you,' said the doctor. 'I wish you good evening.'

Douglas could not resist going up to Professor Cromarty and introducing himself.

'Forgive me, professor,' he said, 'but I was most interested in your interview.'

'Had I known what was going to happen I wouldn't have come,' said the professor.

'Dr Erskine was complaining to me that it was very unjust that my wife should get her prize free of tax after our son had only spent a very short time in filling in a football pool coupon, whereas he had spent three years writing a book and would have to pay heavy taxes on the royalties which he receives in respect of it. He thinks that was grossly unjust and I wondered if you agreed?'

'Unjust to him or on the people who buy the book?' asked Professor Cromarty.

'I inferred that he meant that it was unjust to him.'

'If it's the book I'm thinking of,' said the professor, 'he was very lucky to have found a publisher to publish it at all. I gather you're a librarian?'

'Only fiction, I'm afraid,' said Douglas.

'Well, you might consider putting some of Dr Erskine's literary histories in your library. There are bits of those which are as good bits of fiction as I've ever read. Perhaps I'm wrong in saying "as good". They're as fictional as anything I've ever read.'

'I'm afraid,' said Douglas, 'that the author has to state that the work is fiction for us to put it in the library.'

'You'd never get him to admit anything. As a matter of fact I did once write a novel as a very young man.'

'Just a minute,' said Douglas. 'Wasn't it called *Without Blemish*?'

'You're absolutely right. There's an example of injustice for you. It had superlative reviews and only sold two thousand copies.'

'We have one in the Library,' said Douglas. 'And I'll make a point of reading it.'

'I shouldn't,' said the professor, with unexpected humility. 'It isn't worth reading. But the point is that the critics of the day thought it was.'

'Then why didn't it sell?' asked Douglas. 'Presumably the public of the day thought it wasn't.'

'The public of the day,' said the professor, 'never knew it was on sale. The publishers didn't advertise it and the book-sellers didn't stock it. I quite understand that it's no good advertising a bad book, but all the independent people or most of them said that this was a good book. However, that's past history. I'm merely quoting it as an example of an injustice.'

On the whole the Barton family did not think that the day had gone too badly, but they wondered what would happen in the next few days.

CHAPTER TEN

Distribution

It took a few days for the begging letters to arrive because most of them were sent via Vulgans Pools or the B.B.C. The Bartons' address had not been mentioned, only the district in which they lived. Some people took the trouble to look up their address in a local telephone directory but the majority sent their letters to be forwarded. At the end of a fortnight they had over five hundred letters. Susan separated them into two piles. In the one pile were those which she considered were fraudulent or unworthy and in the other pile were those which she either considered meritorious or where there was a doubt about it.

Douglas sampled the unmeritorious pile but, as he agreed with Susan's view about every letter which he read, he felt it was not necessary to read them all. But Theo and Edward looked at some of them.

One of the letters in the meritorious pile was as follows.

Dear Mrs Barton,

I realise that you will have hundreds of letters and that there will be many people and institutions whom you wish to help out of your prize money. May I first of all congratulate you on your success. I have been trying the pools for many, many years but have never had a dividend at all. So it's no good my saying I'm not envious of your win. Of course I am. It may be that you have decided not to distribute any of your prize money except among people and institutions who are known to you. In that case please do not waste your time reading any more of this.

I am a widower aged 83 living in a little country village and my sole means of support is the old age pension and additional social security benefits when I can get them. I have a roof over my head and enough to eat so that I have no very strong claim upon your kindness. My interests in life are my garden, which includes feeding the birds, reading (we have quite a good public library which comes round once a week), looking at television and writing letters. I suppose that you will have to discount part of the favourable impression which I hope my letter will make upon you by reason of the fact that I am a practised hand. This is not the first letter which I have written asking for assistance by any means. I am occasionally successful but not often. The very simple reason that I am asking for a small donation is one which is well-known to you, the additional cost of everything. But I don't like to let the birds go short and the cost of bird-seed nowadays is almost prohibitive from my point of view. I manage to get by economising on my own food. That is one respect in which you could help me. I have told you what my interests are but in mentioning them I did not mention eating. I'm like most people and food and drink mean a good deal to me. As far as drink is concerned, the most I can afford is a bottle of beer at week-ends. Whisky and gin are unknown in my cottage which a previous owner aptly called Frugal Cottage.

If you could see your way to letting me have a small sum to help me to improve my standard of living for a week or two, or if you felt generous, a few months, I should be most grateful.

I realise that you may think that this letter comes from

a professional beggar and that much or all of what I have told you is untrue, so I have the vicar's permission to tell you that, if you care to write to him or telephone, he would, I think, confirm to you what I have said.

Having seen you on television, I can see you are young enough to have many years in front of you. I hope that they will all be happy ones and happier because of your good fortune. If, as you eat your oysters and drink your champagne, you can spare a thought for me I shall be grateful. But I realise that you will have far more worthy people and causes to support than me and I shall therefore not be aggrieved if you ignore

Yours sincerely,
GREGORY PONSONBY (no relation to the
well-known family)

Douglas telephoned the vicar and explained who he was.

'I'm so sorry to trouble you, vicar,' he said, 'but I have had a letter from one of your parishioners, Gregory Ponsonby, and he said I might speak to you about it.'

'Old Gregory, eh?' said the vicar. 'It doesn't surprise me. What did he say?'

Douglas read out the letter.

'As far as I know,' said the vicar, 'what he says is quite true. He is quite a nice old boy, but he's a confirmed scrounger. He comes to church pretty regularly, but, whether that's because he's genuinely religious or because he'd like my confirmation of the letters which he writes from time to time, such as the one you had, I'm not sure. But he's an honest old boy and I don't think you need feel you'd be doing any harm if you made a small donation.'

'Thank you very much,' said Douglas. 'That's all I wanted to know. I think I'll send him fifty pounds.'

'He'll be delighted. While I'm on the phone, may I take the opportunity of congratulating you and your wife, both of you, on your success. I hope that it will bring you a great deal of happiness.'

'It will help,' said Douglas, 'but you'll be glad to know that we're a happy family anyway.'

'Good,' said the vicar. There was a slight pause. 'I wonder,' he went on, after a few seconds silence, 'whether I might mention a small matter to you?'

'Certainly,' said Douglas.

'D'you happen to know our village?'

'No.'

'Well, we've got a very old church, which although not spectacularly beautiful, is quite attractive both inside and out.'

'I gather,' said Douglas, 'it's badly in need of repair.'

'I can see you have imagination,' said the vicar.

'I'm afraid it didn't require much imagination,' said Douglas. 'Have you opened an appeal fund?'

'As a matter of fact, that is what I was going to be bold enough to mention to you. We are trying to raise five thousand pounds.'

'How much have you raised so far?'

'Only half.'

'I'd be very pleased to send you a small donation, say a hundred pounds,' said Douglas.

'That's exceedingly generous, but just as old Ponsonby referred you to me for confirmation, would you care for me to refer you to the church-wardens or someone else who could satisfy you about the necessity for repairing the church?'

'No, please don't bother,' said Douglas, and added quietly to Sheila, after putting his hand over the mouthpiece, 'It would probably mean further requests from them.'

After thanking the vicar and saying that he would shortly be sending the cheques, Douglas ended the conversation.

'There are several other letters,' said Susan, 'which give you the names of people who could confirm the truth of the contents.'

'It's like a snowball,' said Douglas. 'I think we should avoid asking for confirmation if we can.'

At that moment there was a ring at the bell and Susan answered it and found standing outside a woman of about fifty wearing a man's sweater and corduroy trousers which were muddy and worn.

'I have an appointment to see Mr Barton,' said the lady. 'My name is Penelope Spennell, s – p – e double n-e-double l, but it's pronounced Spenhole, at any rate by me.'

'How did you make the appointment?' asked Susan.

'Through the Lord,' said Mrs Spennell.

'Oh, I see,' said Susan. 'I'm not sure if either Mr or Mrs Barton is available.'

'He said that one of them would be and He's not let me down yet.'

'Would you mind waiting for a moment or two? Do come in and please sit down.'

Susan went quickly to Douglas and Sheila. 'There's a mad woman just arrived,' she said.

'Probably first of many,' said Douglas. 'What does she want?'

'She said that God had made an appointment for you to see her.'

'It's no good our asking for confirmation of that,' said Douglas. 'It'll probably be quicker to see her in the end.'

'There are going to be a lot more of these people,' said Susan, 'and, if you start seeing them, you'll spend half your day at it.'

'You're probably right,' said Douglas, 'but, as this is the first, I think I'll see her. You stay with Sheila. I'll shout if I need any help.'

He went into the entrance hall where Mrs Spennell was sitting down.

'Good morning,' he said. 'I understand you want to see me.'

'God is very good,' said Mrs Spennell.

'We can agree about that.'

'I hope we shall agree about everything.'

'May I ask what it is you want to see me about?'

'Has the Lord not told you?'

'He's given me some sort of an indication. I imagine that you would like some of the money which my wife has just won?'

'That's a very crude way of putting it,' said Mrs Spennell, 'but it is substantially correct. Only you don't put it quite high enough. I would like a lot of the money.'

'For what purpose, may I ask?'

'Didn't He tell you that? That's unlike Him.'

'Perhaps He didn't have the time. You see, we have been rather busy.'

'Surely you can't be so busy that you can't attend to messages from the Lord who made Heaven and earth and you and me and Vulgans Football Pools?'

'No,' said Douglas, 'I'm afraid I only know that you want a lot of the money. Perhaps you could tell me what for?'

'For current expenditure.'

'Expenditure on what?'

'Surely you know about our group?'

'I'm afraid not, Mrs Spennell.'

'Spenhole, if you please.'

'I'm sorry, Mrs Spenhole.'

'Well, we need a house and a sufficient income to supply our needs, which will not be great. There are fifty of us and He has told us to retire. At the same time He said that you would provide for all our needs and naturally we assumed that He'd sent you for the purpose. Did He by any chance mention a hundred thousand pounds? We've worked it out that, after paying for the house, there would be enough capital left to provide for us for the next year or two if the rate of inflation doesn't increase too much.'

'Thank you very much, Mrs Spenhole,' said Douglas. 'If you will leave your name and address we will write to you.'

'When may we expect to receive the cheque?'

'I can't guarantee that there will be a cheque.'

143

'But He said there would be. A large one.'

'We'll let you know,' said Douglas.

'I can't very well go to an estate agent and ask him to buy us a house if I have no firmer assurance than that.'

'No, I shouldn't,' said Douglas. 'You see, we've only just had this money and there are a large number of calls upon it and I'm afraid it will be very doubtful if we shall be able to meet your request.'

'I've never known Him break his word yet.'

'Perhaps you misunderstood it.'

'I've never misunderstood it yet.'

'You say there are fifty of you? Are you sure He didn't tell you to work as hard as you all can, to be as economical as possible in your living and to save up until you can find enough money to carry out your object?'

'What makes you think that?'

'It seems the most sensible thing to have said.'

'In other words, you're turning me down flat.'

'If you think it will save time,' said Douglas, 'yes, I'm afraid I am.'

'You'll regret it,' said Mrs Spennell, 'though not perhaps as much as we shall.'

'I think I did rather well over that,' said Douglas, after Mrs Spennell had gone away. 'I don't quite know what I'd have done if she'd continued to stay and pressed her claim. I think we'd better take it in turns to deal with them. Sheila, you have the next one. Susan can have the one after. But we shouldn't laugh at them really. People who come to us have not only got no money, they've no pride or dignity either. Just look at some of these letters. I'm even sorry for the professional beggars. I wish to God you'd remembered to put that cross in the box, Theo. I simply can't understand how you failed to do it.'

'Nor can I,' said Theo. 'I'm terribly sorry.'

'Here's a letter from a chap I knew in Dartmoor,' said Edward.

'What was he like?'

'Not a bad chap really, but this wasn't his line of country. He used to go after the girls. A good-looking chap with a good figure and a good voice. He would pose as an ex-officer or a baronet or something of that kind. I don't think he's got a wife. I don't think he's ever been married, but he would propose marriage and get as much money out of the girl as he could right up to the wedding day and then disappear. He wasn't terribly successful and they usually found him in the end. He got most of his victims from marriage bureaux and that sort of thing. He must have been having rather a bad time to have to resort to this.'

'What's he say?' asked Douglas.

'Quite a long story. He wants to bring his elderly parents back from Australia because his sister's desperately ill with a mental illness and the doctors have advised that she needs her parents at once. A matter of five hundred pounds.'

'How d'you know it's him?'

'He's written in his own handwriting and has given his real name.'

'It couldn't be true, I suppose?' asked Douglas.

'He never mentioned his parents to me or his sister and I can't think I should have known him so long without some reference being made to Australia. No, I haven't the slightest doubt that this is entirely phoney. But we can ask for confirmation, if you like. It's a rather stupid letter really because it can be proved so easily to be untrue.'

'Suppose it were true,' said Douglas, 'it's the sort of case we might want to help. Ask him for official confirmation from the Australian authorities that his parents exist and want to come to England to see their daughter. If it's a fraud, he won't reply. He can't fake the letters or telegrams.'

'Some people could,' said Edward, 'but I think you're right. He won't be able to. It isn't his line and I don't think you'll hear any more from him.'

'Here's a letter which I think you'll want to see,' said Susan. 'Although it's what I would call a very expensive one.'
It was as follows :

No doubt you will receive many suggestions as to how you should spend your new-found wealth. And you certainly won't be able to adopt all of them. I shall not be in the least surprised if you won't adopt this one, but I hope you will give it a high priority on your list of things which you will want to do for the benefit of the people in this country or at least a few of them.

I am assuming, I hope rightly, that one of the main pleasures you will get out of your enormous win is in distributing it among good causes. If I am wrong about this and you are simply going to buy three Rolls-Royces and go round the World, buy a string of racehorses and have champagne for breakfast, please don't read any more. My letter is not for you.

If, however, you are the sort of person I expect you are – and bear in mind you are not just a name to me but I have seen you on television and your husband and son – I imagine that you will be wondering how you can help those who are less fortunate than yourselves in the present harsh economic conditions. One of the things which the present generation particularly lacks is housing accommodation. How many ordinary young people who get married can find a flat at a reasonable rental? It is difficult to find one at all and now that private landlords cannot normally get rid of tenants whether accommodation is furnished or unfurnished, except on special grounds, the amount of accommodation which is let has been greatly reduced.

My suggestion is that you should spend fifty thousand pounds on buying a site, putting up a building to provide homes for, say, three or four newly married couples. Obviously, if you were prepared to spend a hundred thousand pounds you could do much more, but I doubt whether I would be justified in inviting you to spend so much, bearing in mind the other calls which there will be upon you.

I can provide you with a site and with the names of architects and builders who will carry out my suggestion at an agreed maximum cost. Today this is almost unheard of and builders are going bankrupt because they have agreed to a lump sum contract without providing for the effects of inflation. But for special reasons, which I can explain to you, the people I am concerned with are prepared and able to make their contribution to the welfare of the country by agreeing to a lump sum contract, to include the site and all the work, and the architect is giving his services free. You will obviously want to investigate the suggestion very carefully and I welcome any enquiries which you or your solicitors or accountants may care to ask me. All I hope is that you will give this matter very serious consideration indeed. I don't suppose it would be any attraction to you if I mention that you would of course be able to call the building Barton House or some other title bringing in your name. But might I point out that, while you personally would get no pleasure out of this at all, it might give pleasure to your children or grandchildren or great-grandchildren to know that this was how you spent part of your winnings.

You will of course want to know something about me. I was educated at a public school and Cambridge. I served in the Army during the war without in any way distinguishing myself but at least managing to remain alive. I have supported a wife and three children in reasonable comfort but have too little capital to start a scheme like this of my own. The only other thing which I should perhaps add is that I am in fact the architect to whom I have made reference.

Yours sincerely,
JEREMY FAIRWEATHER

P.S. I have already made plans of the suggested building and, if you think well enough of my proposition to want to see me, I shall be pleased to bring them along to show them to you. Please do not bother to reply if you're not interested. I have other ideas for institutions to house the aged or people who can't keep out of prison. But at the moment I have no sites for such institutions and therefore have not prepared any plans. I could also do a private hospital or a zoo or – and this should appeal to you – a library.

The next few weeks were very hectic for the Bartons. Their house was almost under a state of siege and, in addition to the many strangers who applied to them for support either for themselves or some worthy cause, several on their friends expressly or impliedly called attention to their friendship and some of their acquaintances renewed their acquaintanceship. But they also found that a number of friends and acquaintances kept well away from them. And to their surprise Henry was one of them.

There are people who do not mind loss of dignity if they think that they will get something out of it. There are also people who do not like to appear to be asking. From the point of view of this type of person, while it is perfectly legitimate to congratulate a new member of Parliament on his election, a new judge on his appointment, a couple on their silver wedding or an athlete on breaking a record, he finds it embarrassing and objectionable to congratulate a person on having acquired without any merit at all a large sum of money. Such a person does not like to say that he was delighted to see that Aunt Ethel had left you a hundred thousand pounds or that you had won a seventy-five thousand pounds premium bond. Such letters can only be written by wealthy people who do not need the money for themselves. Douglas and Sheila were surprised to find that Henry came in this category. They were so busy with other matters that they did not notice it for three or four weeks.

Henry had made a habit of coming round to see them at the very least two or three times a month, not always in order to scrounge something, though he was quite prepared to take advantage of the occasion if the opportunity offered. But he genuinely liked them and enjoyed a chat. Now he had kept away from them for a whole month.

'It's very odd,' said Sheila. 'I thought he would be the first to come.'

'Perhaps he's ill,' said Douglas.

'Then Mrs Mountjoy would have wanted some help and she'd soon have been on the telephone to us. I think he's deliberately keeping away from us in case we should think that he had joined the army of beggars. I give him full marks for that.'

Sheila was quite right in thinking that Henry had deliberately kept away from them. He had discussed the matter with Mrs Mountjoy.

'Well,' he had said, while they were talking about the Bartons' new state of affairs, 'there shouldn't be much difficulty in touching them for a bottle of gin in the future. But I think I'll give them a wide berth for the moment. I'd hate them to think I was after their money. That's one thing I've never touched them for. Or anybody else for that matter.'

'What about fumbling for the taxi fare?' said Mrs Mountjoy.

'Yes, I suppose I've done my share of that, but that's rather different. It's all in character. Asking for money is worse than not standing your round of drinks. As a matter of fact I might easily have been one of the scroungers who don't, if I hadn't been taught a lesson at no expense in my early days. I belonged to a pretty convivial golf club and there was one chap who always waited until people really couldn't take any more before he faintly offered another round and said "Won't you really?" almost before they had time to refuse. Half a dozen members got a bit tired of this and they decided to show him up. I happened to be present. It wasn't me, I assure you, but in those days it might have been. "Who's going to pay for the first round?" said the leading conspirator. "I know," said another, "I'll give the word Go and the last person to put both hands on the bar will pay for the drinks. Agreed?" Everyone, including the victim, agreed. "Are you ready?" They were and said so. "Go." The only person who put his hands on the bar was the victim. He was quite an intelligent chap. He paid for the first round, made an excuse for leaving and resigned from the club. You see, I've never forgotten it.'

It was in fact six weeks after the presentation of the cheque that Henry first called round on Douglas and Sheila.

'How are things?' he asked. 'I thought I'd give you a chance to cope before I came round.'

'It's been pretty hectic,' said Douglas, 'but thanks to Sheila and Susan, not to say Edward and Theo, we've managed rather well. I'm glad to say that trade is now dropping. Have a drink.'

'That isn't what I came for,' said Henry, 'but you've never known me refuse yet.'

'What will it be? Gin, whisky or sherry?'

'A little dry sherry, thank you.'

'We've only the one, I'm afraid,' said Douglas, 'but it's not British and it's quite dry.'

'Splendid.'

'I'm glad you've come,' said Sheila, 'because we wanted to ask you rather a difficult question.'

'Fire ahead,' said Henry. For once he looked a little uncomfortable.

'Don't take it the wrong way,' said Sheila, 'but there's no fun in having a win like we've had, unless our friends get fun out of it too. Is there anything we can do for you?'

'This sherry is awfully good,' said Henry. 'How very kind of you. For once I assure you that I haven't come scrounging. I've decided not to, as a matter of fact.'

'It would give us all the more pleasure. We wondered if you wanted a new bathroom or a new car or something of that kind? Or, to put it more crudely, whether you could do with the cash.'

'I suppose,' said Henry, 'there are very few people today who would say No to that, but quite frankly I'd prefer something in kind. A small new car would be a wonderful present to have. It would be a continuing reminder of your kindness.'

'That's bad,' said Douglas. 'That's the way to lose friends.'

'I suppose,' said Sheila, 'he couldn't help being reminded of it when he takes it in for repair after the first week.'

'And eventually has to return it to the makers after the first month,' said Douglas. 'Yes, I suppose you're right there. Anyway, Henry, think over what you'd like and we do assure you that it would give Sheila and me the greatest pleasure to see you driving it. But do remember that, if you should have some dreadful calamity in which you do need some financial assistance, don't hesitate to come to us.'

'I don't suppose you'll have any left,' said Henry. 'I expect that you've spent the last few weeks giving it away as fast as you can.'

'We have given away a good deal, but we've kept enough to look after ourselves and our friends if they need any.'

This in fact had not been easy. Aunt Agatha's fifty thousand pounds had in a way set the standard of distribution rather too high, and when they only gave away five thousand pounds they felt it was inconsiderable. They gave much larger amounts on the lines of their gift to Aunt Agatha to various institutions and before long they had finally disposed of four-fifths of their winnings. When they bore in mind the heavy taxation which their capital and income would incur, the cost of keeping the girls at school and providing for their further education in advance, a hundred thousand pounds did not seem to be too large a sum, even if some old acquaintance did not come round to say that he was going to go bankrupt unless a little loan of twenty-five thousand pounds could be obtained.

CHAPTER ELEVEN

The Conjuring Trick

After six months Sheila and Douglas were able to settle down to a very happy form of life, they were able to withdraw the security guards protecting their daughters and themselves and the publicity had long ceased to affect them. And although they still looked back with horror upon some of the things which they had had to do and endure, they were unquestionably most grateful for the success which they'd had. It had completely altered their lives and they were now able to live happily and comfortably without having to worry where the money was going to come from. Financial worry had been their only problem before their big win and now they had no problems at all. In short, no family could have been made happier by a win on the pools or have made better use of their winnings than the Bartons.

It was about a year after they had been enjoying their new life that they gave a party at their cottage at which they had arranged for a kind of imitation Uri Geller to give a performance. The entertainer was hugely successful but from Theo's point of view the conjuror was too pleased with his success. He in fact did some wonderful tricks and no one there could possibly tell how they were done, but Theo resented his vanity and even more his pretence that his tricks were done by virtue of extrasensory perception or some magical gift which he alone possessed. He called himself the Man of the Spirit and, introducing his first trick, he said :

'Ladies and gentlemen, I am delighted that you invited me to perform before you this afternoon. I hope that you will enjoy my performance, which I might add I have given before I won't say all the crowned heads of Europe because there aren't enough of them – but before prominent men and women all over the world, including the greatest scientists, technologists and some of the most eminent statesmen and politicians – I don't pause to state the difference – before highbrows and lowbrows, before intellectuals and down-to-earth business men. None of them, so far as I know, has been able to discover how I do what in fact I do. And this is hardly surprising because I am the only person who knows. I do not claim any credit for being able to give the entertainment which is to follow. I could not run a mile under four minutes. Probably I could not run it under ten. But I venture to claim that Sir Roger Bannister could not do any of the things that I am about to do or tell you how they were done. Now Sir Roger Bannister does deserve credit for having been the first man to run a mile in four minutes because he devoted a very large amount of time to the necessary physical training to enable him to do it. But he deserves no credit for having been born with a body which enabled him to do these things. Similarly, I deserve no credit whatever for having been given the mind to enable me to do what I do. I claim the same credit for myself as Sir Roger Bannister could claim for himself and no more. Power is in the mind and if you have a mind sufficiently powerful, as I venture to think I have, there is practically nothing that you cannot do. I do not claim that I can actually move mountains, but I can do things almost as spectacular and I am going to show you some of them tonight. There is one thing I must add before I start. Mr and Mrs Barton have commissioned me to give this entertainment. They will confirm to you that I have never seen them before, nor –' and he looked carefully round the room – 'nor have I seen before any of the audience who are now in this room. First of all, I should like to be corrected if I am wrong. Does anyone in this room dispute what I have said?'

There was no answer.

'Now, although I have only just come here and know none of you, of course it would always be possible in a short space of time for me to arrange with one of you to be a confederate. For example, when I was staying at an hotel once where I knew no one and had not yet met the manager, on a wet afternoon he was entertaining some of the guests by doing some card tricks. I had only just come into the room and was sitting at the end of the table. The trick he was about to do was one in which he put a number of cards face down on the table, told his audience that he would go out of the room and that, while he was out of the room, they should either touch one or more of the cards or not touch any of them and he would come back and tell them whether they'd touched any of them and which. As he passed me on his way out he whispered out of the corner of his mouth, "When I come to a card, cough," and out he went. I was the only person who heard or noticed the whisper. Now he was relying entirely upon the sporting instinct of the British public. How could I let him down? Of course I couldn't and I didn't. He pretended partly that he could tell from the feel of a card or from the warmth of somebody's fingers which had touched it. Of course it was all done by me. I gave him full marks. He took a chance but it was a very small one. Now I want to get the assurance of everyone here that I haven't done the same thing. And that in fact, except for a small conversation about my journey here and that sort of thing, when Mr and Mrs Barton welcomed me into their home, I have spoken to no one here. Does anyone dispute this?' Again no one did.

'Very well then. I will start. Please do not say, when I have finished, that I have a confederate in the room. Now, having said that I haven't a confederate in the room, my first action is to ask for one. Would someone please come up here and examine this pack of cards?'

After he had gone through most of his repertoire he was incautious enough to ask if anyone had seen any of his feats carried out by someone else. There was silence for a few moments and then Theo said :

'As a matter of fact, I have.'

The entertainer was not pleased. 'So you have, have you?' he said. 'Could you do them yourself by any chance?'

'Not without training,' said Theo.

'Oh, you could do them with training, could you? You don't accept that what I said in the first instance was true, that it is all done through the mind, in this case my mind.'

'I'd rather not answer that question,' said Theo.

'Oh please do. I'm sure the audience would like to hear.'

'If you really insist,' said Theo, 'no, I don't. I think they're all tricks. No doubt performed with great dexterity and charm and with one hundred per cent success, but in my opinion they are all tricks.'

The performer was rather nettled. 'Perhaps you could do something like them?' he said.

'Yes, I should think so,' said Theo.

'Could you give us all the opportunity of seeing it? I'm sure the audience would be delighted.'

'It's your show and not mine, but if you'd all like me to –' said Theo. The response by the audience was obviously encouraging, so Theo began.

'I haven't got our guest's patter and I've not performed this trick before any of the crowned heads of Europe or anything like that. In fact I've only once done it before, so I hope it will come off. I'll tell you what I'm going to do. I'm going to get a bottle of ink and a pen and two pieces of paper. I'm going to ask two members of the audience, who, I hope, will confirm that they are not confederates, to assist me. Indeed perhaps our guest will choose two members of the audience. I will go out of the room and, when I return, I shall ask them to write a word or their name or something short on a piece of paper.'

Theo went out of the room and the conjuror chose two members of the audience to assist him in the trick. Theo came back with a bottle of ink and two pens and two pieces of paper, each about two inches by four inches in size.

'Before I start I would like our guests to examine the pen and the ink to be satisfied that they are just the normal sort of thing you use in everyday life.' The conjuror could see that it was ordinary ink and an ordinary pen and said he would take Theo's word for it.

'Very well then,' said Theo, and he turned to the people who were going to assist him. 'Would you each write a word, please, on this piece of paper.' And he handed a piece to each of them. 'You can do it in full view of the audience and I shall see the word you write.'

One man wrote down his name, Robinson, and the other wrote down the word 'crafty'.

'Thank you,' said Theo. 'Show those pieces of paper to the audience and wait until they're dry.' This was done. 'Now,' said Theo, 'I will place them face down on the table and put a book over each of them. The trick is simply this. I have to be alone while I do it, so I'll go out of the room, but I'm going to make each of those pieces of paper blank again.' He turned to the conjuror, 'D'you think you could do that?'

'Let's see you do it first.'

'You shall,' said Theo. He went out of the room and there was a buzz of conversation for a few minutes until he returned.

'Now, Mr Robinson,' he said, 'would you kindly take the book off your piece of paper, turn it over and exhibit it to the audience?' Mr Robinson did so and the sheet was as blank as it was before he had written his name upon it.

'And now, Mrs Prendergast?' Mrs Prendergast lifted up the

book and turned over the paper and where the word 'crafty' had been written there was absolutely nothing at all. There was considerable applause.

Douglas did not join in the applause. He suddenly had an appalling thought. It was so appalling that he felt that he could not wait to find out if his suspicion was right. Accordingly, as soon as he decently could, without appearing discourteous to his guests, he closed down the proceedings and bade them all goodbye. Before he left, the conjuror spoke to Douglas.

'Very clever that trick of your son's,' he said. 'You know how it was done, I suppose?'

'How was it done?' asked Douglas.

'Quite obviously, sleight of hand.'

'How d'you mean? said Douglas. 'I saw nothing.'

'Of course not, nor did I, even though I'm an expert. It was quite brilliantly done. But what happened was this. When he placed the pieces of paper under the books, he obviously substituted two similar pieces of paper.'

'It was as simple as that, was it?' said Douglas.

'Yes,' said the conjuror, 'but it was well done, really well done.'

He turned to Theo. 'I congratulate you. You could make a living at this,' he said. 'You must practise a good deal with your fingers.'

'Have you, Theo?' asked Douglas.

'As a matter of fact, I haven't,' said Theo.

'Well, I congratulate you. What was particularly good was that the paper on which the words were written was simply paper, not cardboard. Much much difficult to hold and move.'

'You're quite sure,' said Douglas, 'that that was the way it was done?'

'Certainly. It couldn't have been done in any other way. The converse could be done with invisible ink. You know. You write something which doesn't appear on the paper until it's warm or something of that sort. Or it can be done by time. Some ink will only show itself after so many minutes on the paper. That I've often seen done. But I've never seen the ink disappear before. And when you find that a thing that can't happen happening you know there's only one way in which it could happen. That is by sleight of hand.'

'Why not by the power of the mind?' asked Theo. 'That's how you do your trick.'

'I can only say,' said the conjuror, 'that you did not remove that ink by the power of *your* mind. Now I really must be going.'

When the conjuror and all the guests had gone, Douglas took Theo for a walk in the garden.

'I want you to set my mind at rest,' he said. 'Was that sleight of hand?'

Theo did not answer. 'As a matter of fact—,' he eventually began and then hesitated. For so long that his father said: 'Yes?'

'No, it wasn't.'

'So you've invented something,' said his father, 'which enables you to take the ink off paper. Does it enable you to put it back again?'

Theo did not answer.

'Theo,' said Douglas, 'you must tell me. I've always known that you were a brilliant inventor and that one day you might produce something quite stupendous. Now I have a nasty feeling that I wish you weren't so brilliant. I can't tell you the relief I had for a moment when the conjuror said that you'd done it by sleight of hand. I wish to God you had.'

Theo said nothing.

'You must know what I'm talking about, Theo,' said Douglas. 'We must have this out. I'm afraid your silence has confirmed my suspicions. For Heaven's sake show me that I'm wrong if I am. But don't keep me in suspense. You knew that your mother and I were very hard up and you must have heard us talking about our difficulties in going on paying the fees for the girls. You knew that all that could be put right if we won a football pool. Have you invented something which enabled us to win it?'

'I've never lied to you or Mother on any serious matter,' said Theo 'and I can't now. Yes, I did.'

'What did you actually do?'

'You know the way in which aeroplanes and ships can be controlled by wireless by remote control. I used to annoy you with mine. I found I could do the same with ink. I would make some ink radioactive and responsive to the call of my transmitter. In fact I could have made that ink visible again. What I did was to fill in a coupon in the permutation column where you choose ten matches and, if any eight of those ten are draws, you win. That costs 22½p, which is what Mother had been staking. In fact I put a cross against every match but all but ten of them I blotted out with my transmitter in the first instance. So that, when Vulgans received the coupon, it looked like a normal entry with simply ten crosses in the column. You remember that I spent several week-ends away from home. The first week-end I just tried it out and, as soon as the results of the matches were known, I wiped out enough crosses and put in enough to ensure that Mum won a fifth prize. When I found that she did, I knew that the thing worked and that the pools company had nothing to prevent it. Once they knew of such an invention they could easily take steps to protect themselves. For example, they could puncture every cross on every coupon as soon as it arrived, or they could take photostats of every coupon. It would cost a certain amount of money, but as the customers pay for that, it wouldn't hurt the pools company. But I imagined, rightly as it turned out, that in the first instance the only thing for which the coupons were checked was the time of delivery. I went up in my car and parked myself near Vulgans' premises and, as soon as the results came in on the wireless in my car, I proceeded to use my transmitter to alter Mum's coupon until it had eight draws. I wouldn't have done it that week if it hadn't been a good week, but it happened to be an excellent one where there were only eight draws.'

'In other words,' said Douglas, 'we've obtained half a million pounds by fraud.'

'Not your fraud, Dad, mine.'

'But now that I know about it, what the devil am I going to do?'

'I'm terribly sorry, Dad,' said Theo. 'I oughtn't to have told you. It was very stupid of me to do that trick, but that fellow riled me and I thought I'd show him something. Unfortunately, I've shown it to you too. Oh, just one rather amusing thing,' said Theo, 'if anything can be amusing in these circumstances.'

'What?' said Douglas.

'Well, I did put a cross in the no publicity box, but by accident in erasing some of the other crosses I erased that one too.'

CHAPTER TWELVE

The Problem of Conscience

The situation of the Bartons now was far worse than if they had never had their half million pounds. There were so many problems to be solved. Douglas and Sheila discussed the matter at some length while Theo was in his workshop.

'With our savings we've a hundred thousand pounds we can return to them,' said Douglas. 'But that's only a fifth of what we had. And if we did return that to them, what could we say? We'd have to explain how we got the money and that would involve Theo. They'd almost certainly prosecute him and he'd probably go to prison for some years.'

'Then we can't tell them,' said Sheila.

'But we may be guilty of an offence by keeping the hundred thousand pounds now that we know how it was obtained.'

'I can't help it,' said Sheila. 'We're not going to do anything that will give Theo away. We're not having a son of ours sent to prison.'

'I think we'd better go and see old Stockwell at once,' said Douglas. 'Come with me tomorrow afternoon. I'll try and make an appointment for my lunch time.'

The following day Douglas and Sheila went to the offices of their solicitors, Messrs Stockwell & Son, and saw the senior partner, whom they had known for many years and who was something of a friend. Douglas explained to him what had happened.

'Are you quite sure he's not dreamed it up?' said Stockwell. 'It's such an extraordinary thing to be able to do.'

'Theo is an inventor,' said Douglas, 'and I'm quite satisfied from what he has said to me that in fact he altered the coupon while it was in the possession of Vulgans. That's why we came to you as soon as we knew about it. What on earth are we to do?'

'Quite a problem,' said Stockwell. 'The money was unquestionably obtained by the fraud of your son. Both of you were of course completely innocent in the matter, but, if you keep this hundred thousand pounds, it can be said that you are guilty of stealing it if you don't return it to the owners, now that you know it was obtained from them by fraud.'

'We could send them the money anonymously, 'said Sheila.

'That would, I think, clear you. No prosecution could succeed against you if you did that. But it wouldn't clear up the matter altogether.'

'You mean the other four hundred thousand pounds?' asked Douglas.

'Of course there's that, but I didn't mean that for the moment. You see, although legally it's Vulgans who've been defrauded, they haven't lost a penny. The people who've been cheated are the people who would have won the prize if your coupon hadn't been altered. There may be half a dozen of them and, if there were, it would mean that each would have lost about eighty thousand pounds or so less the prize which they actually got. Now, if you send a hundred thousand pounds back to the pools company purely anonymously without saying why it's been sent or for what week it's being sent, they won't have the faintest idea to whom to distribute the money so that, although it would clear you of dishonesty, it won't put the matter right in any degree. In fact, all it will do is to make Vulgans richer by a hundred thousand pounds. So if you're interested in the moral as well as the legal side, sending them back that money will be of no use whatever.'

'It makes things very awkward,' said Douglas, 'because any attempt by us to find out who ought to have had the money cannot be made without calling attention to the week in which the money was won. That will result in Vulgans making enquiries from us. We should then either have to lie or give Theo away.'

'If it's a choice between the two,' said Sheila, 'I'm quite prepared to lie, but of course I don't want to. Theo's had practically none of the money for himself. He only did it to help us and, although it was very wrong of him, there was a very good motive for his behaviour.'

'If you could be more of a layman than a lawyer for the moment,' said Douglas, 'which do you consider is our greater moral duty? To protect our son or to see that the people who should have had the prize money get it? Or at any rate part of it? What would you do in the same position?'

Stockwell thought for a moment and then said : 'It's rather difficult for me. You see I'm a lawyer and I should feel bound to disclose the true facts to the pool promoters.'

'Even at the cost of your son going to prison?'

'I'm afraid so. I repeat that may well be because I'm a lawyer, but I don't for a moment say that I'm right. As a solicitor I'm not concerned so much with moral values as with legal duties.'

'What do you advise us to do?'

'I think that as a solicitor I'm bound to advise you to tell the whole story to Vulgans and at the same time pay back the hundred thousand pounds and state to whom the rest of the money was distributed. You see, they may be able to get some of that back if it hasn't been spent. No doubt you've given a lot to charities. If the money can be traced in their accounts and has not yet been spent, it could probably be recovered from them by Vulgans.'

'How perfectly awful,' said Sheila. 'And the same applies to individuals, I suppose?'

'Certainly. If an individual, for example, to whom you gave two thousand pounds had bought a car with that money, Vulgans could claim the car. In other words, if the money is still in somebody's account or can be traced to some specific article, Vulgans could get it back from them.'

'What a mess,' said Douglas.

'It is indeed,' said Stockwell, 'and I wish there were some useful advice that I could give you. Obviously everything you've said to me is in complete confidence, so that, if you don't take my advice as a solicitor, no harm will come to Theo or to anybody else. But I repeat that I am bound to advise you that your legal duty as the people who obtained the money from Vulgans is to go and tell them how it was obtained, to repay all that you have left of it and to tell them how you expended the rest of it.'

'D'you think that, if we did that, there's any chance that they wouldn't prosecute Theo?'

'I'm afraid I don't,' said Stockwell. 'I suppose that, if you were able to restore to them the complete half million so that they could distribute it among the lawful prizewinners, they might be prepared not to prosecute in view of the return of the money and your and your son's frankness in admitting how it was obtained. That is a possibility but by no means a certainty. You see, it's no small thing to obtain half a million pounds by fraud. I'm sorry to have to call it that, but that's what it is.'

'There's no point in discussing that last suggestion,' said Douglas, 'because there's no hope whatever of our raising the other four hundred thousand pounds. And even if we went to some of the people who've had it, it's about a year since we gave it to them and a lot of it is bound to be gone. And what'll happen if we don't accept your advice?'

'Nothing,' said Stockwell. 'No one knows about this except

you and Theo and me. Vulgans haven't the faintest idea that it's happened. And no one will be any the wiser if you use up the whole of the hundred thousand pounds you've got left. But I'm bound to point out to you that that will not only be morally wrong but legally wrong too. You'd be committing a very serious offence by doing it.'

'So it boils down to this,' said Douglas, 'that at least we must send the hundred thousand pounds back anonymously. That will do no harm to Theo and is our own legal and moral duty. If we have a moral duty to do more than that and if the discharge of that duty would result in Theo being prosecuted, I think our moral duty to him is greater than our moral duty to the other competitors. They won't know what they've lost. But obviously we must send a hundred thousand pounds back as quickly as we can. How d'you think it could best be done? Should we get you to do it or should we just get a banker's draft and post it to them anonymously?'

'If you're quite determined not to do anything more than that, I think that you should do it yourselves and in cash,' said Stockwell. 'It's quite true that they wouldn't know who my client was and that I'd refuse to give them any information about it, but they would have something to go on, namely my firm's name, and, for example, they might employ a private detective to get someone into my office as a secretary or something, look up the papers and then they'd have your name. And today with all the industrial spying and bugging and so forth which goes on I think that from that point of view Vulgans should be given no lead at all. Moreover, as a banker's draft for a hundred thousand pounds isn't obtained every hour it would be as well to send the money entirely in cash, so then the only thing they'd have would be the postmark. You could send it by registered post from a large post office out of your district. Send it in a parcel so that it looks like a book, put the notes in a cardboard box or something of that sort. Perhaps you might ask them to acknowledge receipt in the personal column of *The Times*. They may not do so, but they probably will. It would be dangerous to insure the package for a hundred thousand pounds because that would be so unusual that the man who issued the policy might very well recognise you, and you would have to give a name and address.'

'Thank you very much,' said Douglas. 'I think we'll take your advice.'

'If there's anything further,' said Stockwell, 'don't hesitate to get in touch with me. I'm extremely sorry you find yourselves in such a horrible position for no fault whatever of your own. A remarkable young man, your son. I wonder what he'll be inventing next.'

That evening Theo asked them where they'd been and they told him that they had been to see Stockwell and what he'd advised them.

'What a mess I've landed you in,' said Theo. 'That shows the danger of meddling in other people's affairs. Unless I can think of some alternative, you're going to be much worse off than before I started and you've got all this worry in addition. As a matter of fact when I did it, although of course I knew it was wrong, for some extraordinary reason I didn't feel as though I were committing a criminal offence. I knew I was, of course, but it just seemed almost a bit of fun. After all, no one was being cheated in the way of business. No one would know he'd been cheated. The people who didn't get the first prize would have got quite a good second prize, probably several thousands or so, and they wouldn't be worrying. In any event, they were only gambling themselves. As a matter of fact I did more hard work to win the pools that week than anybody else. After all, I spent many hours on this invention. Most of the people who do the pools just choose the teams at random, but, even when they do it by form and all that sort of thing, at the most they only take a few hours. This invention has taken me months to perfect, years you might say because it's come from other things. The trouble is that by itself it isn't much use to anybody, except for cheating or doing conjuring tricks, so I've never really felt the matter on my conscience until now. All I thought was that you badly needed the money and that here was a brilliant way of getting it without any deserving person being any the worse off. But, when it's put to you that I've obtained half a million pounds for you by fraud, it sounds much worse. It also sounds like several years in prison if I were found out. And Edward put me off that at our first meeting. He gave me a complete description of what happens to a man from the time he's convicted for the first time until he finds himself in prison. It's absolutely horrifying.'

'You're not going to prison,' said Douglas.

'I suppose I ought really,' said Theo. 'It's true I didn't get away with as much as the train robbers. But quite a number of people have got sentences of many years for robbing the banks of less than I got from Vulgans. When are you going to send the money back?'

'Tomorrow or the next day, if possible. As soon as we can.'

'It's a pity you can't wait for a bit, but I'll be making criminals of you if you do.'

'Why d'you say that?'

'I must try and think up something. After all, I got you into this and it's up to me to get you out.'

'I think we must send the money back at once,' said Douglas. 'Now that we know that we're not entitled to it, if we hang on to it, according to Stockwell, it's equivalent to stealing. And stealing a hundred thousand pounds is quite an offence, even with inflation.'

'I tell you what,' said Theo, 'you let me have the hundred thousand pounds and I'll send it off.'

'Why should you?'

'It's quite a nuisance for you to have to make the necessary arrangements with the bank. I'll collect it and send it off. First things first. Then you'll be in the clear. After that, I'll see what can be done about the balance.'

Theo was completely trusted by his parents and they agreed to his suggestion.

Later that evening Edward spoke to Theo.

'Don't answer this if you'd rather not, but I couldn't help hearing a few words spoken between you and your father and of course I was present at the party, so putting two and two together, I think I know what's happened. I wonder if I can help in any way?'

'First of all,' said Theo, 'what d'you think's happened?'

'To put it crudely, I think you're responsible for your mother winning that half a million pounds.'

'But of course. I filled in the coupon.'

'I don't mean that,' said Edward. 'I think you worked it with one of your inventions. Your parents must be in a flat spin, because you could get at least three years for that, if not five.'

'You obviously know,' said Theo, 'but there's nothing we can do about it, is there?'

'I'd like to be sure,' said Edward, 'that you and your parents don't have a rush of morals to the head and go and make a clean breast of it. Your parents won't if you don't, because they wouldn't dream of doing anything which would result in your going to gaol. I have a nasty feeling that you might do something stupid.'

'I've done that already,' said Theo. 'I've landed them in all this. I'd certainly do anything I could to get them out of it. '

'Your going to prison won't get them out of it,' said Edward. 'On the contrary, it will make it very much worse.'

'Yes, I see that,' said Theo. 'I have an idea or two but it's such a pity the thing's come up now. I want a bit of extra time.'

'How long?'

'A couple of months might do it.'

'That reminds me,' said Edward. 'I wanted to ask a favour. Could I have a fortnight's holiday?'

'Of course. I've offered it to you before, but you've always refused to go. When would you like it?

'Now, as a matter of fact.'

'Today, d'you mean?'

'If that wouldn't be a nuisance.'

'Of course. I can manage very easily.'

'Splendid, then I'll pack a few things and be off. D'you know where Susan is? I'd like to say goodbye to her first.'

CHAPTER THIRTEEN

Susan and Edward

Although Susan had only been engaged temporarily, she had made herself so useful and they liked her so much that Douglas and Sheila felt that they couldn't part with her. She was almost part of the family. They did not know it, but, if they had got rid of Susan, Edward would have left too. He had made up his mind that she was the person he wanted as a lifeline. After a few months' close association they became fond of each other and Susan quickly realised that he might ask her to marry him. She had no difficulty in deciding that, however much she liked him, it was much too early for her to take such a step. He had not been long out of prison and, even if he never went there again, marriage with a man who had at least five convictions for serious crime was not an enterprise to be embarked upon lightly. Indeed, she was far from certain that she could enter upon it at all. However fond she might become of him, it would always be slightly embarrassing to her. When they met strangers and the question of crime and imprisonment arose, the conversation could be extremely awkward. Although Edward might want anybody who was likely to become a close friend to know about his past at an early stage, such information was not to be bandied about to strangers. So, if she married him, she would have to resign herself to the fact that there would inevitably from time to time be occasions of embarrassment.

170

But more important than that was the problem of children. In the first place, would they inherit Edward's tendencies? Although highly respectable men have been the offspring of criminal parents and highly respectable parents have produced criminals, Susan, without having read a great deal about the subject, felt that there was a good deal in breeding.

And then there was a further problem. Was it fair to the children to let them be brought into the world with the knowledge (which they would have to acquire some time) that their father had been a criminal? The corny reply to the schoolboy's question 'What's your father do?', 'At the moment he's doing twelve months,' was too much of a real possibility to be amusing.

Susan was an ordinary, cheerful girl of well above average intelligence but, as she became fonder of Edward, she realised that she must come to some kind of decision. So she compromised. She decided that there must be no question of marriage for a year or two. Quite likely they would go different ways before that period was up and in that way the decision would be made for her. In the meantime, if he should want to make love to her, she would let him do so. And if this happened, Susan decided that, if at the end of two or three years of being lovers, they were desperately fond of each other, she would marry him if that was what he wanted. She recognised that it was a selfish decision and could be unfair to their unborn children. But when she weighed up all the possible vicissitudes in life and drew up a moral balance sheet, she felt that the assets side of the business would be quite considerable, and that the decision need not unduly weigh on her conscience.

She made the decision after she had been with the Bartons for about six months and, in view of this, it was not altogether surprising that within a month after she had made it, she and Edward had become lovers. It was not always easy to achieve their object. Sometimes they had to use the workshop, when Theo was away for the day and Susan wasn't wanted by

Douglas or Sheila. They made it as comfortable as possible and only occasionally gave the game away to Theo by forgetting to take away an odd cushion. Theo said nothing to his parents because he did not see why he should interfere. Nor did he think that they would particularly mind.

But when the blow fell, Edward realised that Douglas and Sheila would have to get rid of Susan almost at once, unless she could afford to stay with them for nothing. And he knew that they would not allow that. Theo had suggested that, if he had a month or two, he might be able to solve the problem. This obviously meant that he hoped that he was near completion of the invention which would in some respect – though in what respect he had no idea – revolutionise the upkeep of the roads. But it was plain that Douglas and Sheila would return the hundred thousand pounds at least some weeks before Theo perfected his invention.

Edward realised that the receipt of the hundred thousand pounds by Vulgans would make them investigate the matter extremely carefully. They would soon arrive at the conclusion that it was very likely that the money came from the winner of a half million pound prize. There were not so many of those and, if they investigated each one, they would soon find out who was responsible. So he decided that he must try to forestall this.

He went up to Birmingham the same day, having previously asked if he could have an interview with the head of the security division. When he arrived he was shown in to Mr McManus.

'What can I do for you?' he was asked, after he had been introduced by the clerk who brought him in.

'I've come about a very serious matter,' he said, 'but I don't expect you to take my word for it until tomorrow morning or maybe the day after that. Certainly within a few days.'

'What is going to happen within a few days?'

'You will receive a hundred thousand pounds in cash without any indication of the name or whereabouts of the sender.'

'I take it that you haven't sent it?'

'No.'

'May I ask the source of your knowledge?'

'I'm afraid I'm not prepared to divulge it, but there is something I will tell you about myself. You have my name. You can check this if you want to, though I should prefer that you didn't at the moment. I have five convictions for fraud against me and on the last occasion I served three years' imprisonment. I came out a little over a year ago. Now, at the moment,' he went on, 'the unlikely story that I have told you about the hundred thousand pounds, coupled with the fact that I am an ex-gaolbird, will make you so doubtful of the truth of what I've told you that you will probably think it better to have another interview with me after you've received the hundred thousand pounds. So I won't say any more at present, except that I shall be staying at the Windsor Hotel under the name I have given you. Perhaps you would be good enough to ring me up in a day or two as soon as you have received the money? But I do ask you not to communicate with the police at the moment. I'm not trying to make any bargain with you but I should tell you that I may be able to be of considerable help to you and accordingly I hope that you will comply with my wishes about communicating with the police at the moment.'

'All right,' said Mr McManus. 'Without binding myself I shall wait until after our next interview, which,' he added, 'I hope will be very soon.'

'It may well be tomorrow,' said Edward before leaving.

It was in fact two days later that Edward received a telephone call from Mr McManus saying that the money had arrived and would he please come and see him immediately at the office.

Edward did as he was asked and within an hour of receiving the telephone call he was in conversation with Mr McManus.

'This is conscience money, I imagine?'

'No,' said Edward. 'I can tell you this, that the sender of that money is a person of the highest character and completely innocent of any misbehaviour, let alone any crime in relation to that hundred thousand pounds.'

'Presumably, though, this hundred thousand pounds was obtained from us by some kind of fraud.'

'But not by the person who sent you the money,' said Edward.

'Then the person who sent it was not aware of the fraud and, when he became aware of it, he immediately sent the money back?'

'That is correct,' said Edward.

'What are we to do with it is the problem. Can you help us in regard to that? This money ought to have been paid to other competitors. If we don't know when the money was obtained, we have no means of sending the money to the people who ought to have had it. Is that what you could help us about?'

'I could,' said Edward, 'but at the moment I don't want to do so.'

'May I ask why you've come here at all? Are you expecting some reward for the information you have given or are going to give us? Are you seeking to avoid prosecution for someone who committed a fraud upon us? Or what other object have you in mind?'

'I will tell you quite frankly. I have already told you that the person who sent you this money back is absolutely innocent of any wrong-doing. It is possible that you will receive further money. Supposing you receive the full amount which was obtained and suppose I can satisfy you that the way in which it had been obtained had nothing whatever to do with your own employees, or anyone in the Post Office, without making any promises, do you think it likely or unlikely that you will try to investigate the matter so as to see that the person responsible for the fraud is prosecuted?'

'How can I answer that question without knowing more of the facts? You suggest that none of our employees is implicated, but, until I know how the fraud was carried out, how can I be sure that that's true?'

'I see that. But suppose you were told how the fraud was carried out and how a similar fraud could be prevented in the future, and suppose the full amount of money which was paid out by you was returned, would there be any good reason why you should pursue your enquiries further? Now, let me make it plain that I am making no admissions myself at all, but I am in a position to tell you how the fraud was carried out. However I am not prepared to do this, if the probability is that you will try to find out the identity of the person responsible.'

'We should probably succeed if we tried,' said Mr McManus. 'We usually do. Even with the information which we now have, apart from what you've given us, it is extremely likely that we should find out all about it. You see, there aren't many prizes of a hundred thousand pounds or more. If we investigated every prize winner who received such a prize in the last two years, I think we should probably arrive at the truth. You must realise, Mr Livermore, that a hundred thousand pounds is a lot of money, We, in a sense, are trustees for the public. We have a record for absolute integrity and we are trusted completely, so we feel that we mustn't let them down.'

'If you got all the money back and were able to prevent such a fraud happening in the future, you wouldn't be letting them down. Particularly if you knew how to distribute the money you got back. I can help you about all those things, and this will save you the expense of very considerable enquiries which in the end might not serve your object.'

'How was the fraud perpetrated?'

'I'm not prepared to tell you that,' said Edward, 'until I have some kind of statement from you as to what action you are likely to take. I repeat that I am not asking for a binding assurance but I am simply asking you what the probable action of your Board would be on a matter like this. I presume you would have to get instructions from the Board when so much is involved?'

Mr McManus thought for about half a minute.

'Well,' he said, 'if we can put the clock back, not within an hour or two or a minute or two or a second or two, but put it back completely – in other words if the total amount of money obtained is repaid and if we are told exactly how it was done and how it can be prevented in the future, then if that did not involve any of our own employees or any of their relatives or friends or anyone in the Post Office, I think it possible that the Board would be prepared to let the matter rest.'

'In return for that,' said Edward, 'I will give you some advice which will enable you to prevent this particular fraud from ever recurring again. It will cost you a certain amount to carry out the advice but that's unavoidable.'

'What is your advice?'

'At some stage before the matches are played every cross on every coupon, except those which ask for no publicity, should be punctured. Another way would be to photostat every coupon before the matches are played. I assume that puncturing each cross would be cheaper than that.'

'You imply,' said Mr McManus, 'that the coupon was already in our possession before the matches were played and somehow or other it was altered without any of our employees being involved.'

'You're quite right,' said Edward, 'that is exactly what happened.'

'But it's impossible,' said Mr McManus. 'We know all about invisible ink and all that sort of thing but if we receive the coupon, duly filled in before the matches are played, the only way in which that competitor would appear to have a correct entry is if a coupon were substituted by someone here.'

'I know that it sounds like that,' said Edward, 'but it is not in fact the case. Although, as I have said, I make no admission of guilt, I could show you exactly how it was done.'

'Well, show me then,' said Mr McManus.

'I can't at the moment. I'd have to get the necessary equipment. I'm prepared to make that part of the bargain – and don't misunderstand me when I say bargain. I know there can't be a legal bargain. But as with your own pools there can be a bargain in honour. And I shall be very happy to accept that, so if your Board will indicate that, on the conditions you've mentioned, there will be no further enquiry into the matter, still less any attempt at a prosecution, I shall be prepared to prove to you in this office exactly how the fraud was perpetrated – and could be again unless you take the precautions which I have told you.'

'When are these further monies likely to be received by us?'

'I can't be sure of that,' said Edward, 'Indeed, it is conceivable that they won't be.'

'If they are not,' said Mr McManus, 'I'm afraid full enquiries will be instituted.'

'If you're going to do that, I don't see why I should give you the further information about the method by which this was done. We both know that there can be no legal bargain of any kind, but some business does not rely upon legalities. It's the only business in the world where millions of pounds are staked and change hands and, as you put in your coupons, it is a matter of honour between the parties only. I should have thought that that was just the sort of business to come to an arrangement about this matter which should be satisfactory to everyone.'

'It won't be satisfactory to the people who should have been the prize-winners on the occasion in question.'

'They no doubt got a prize,' said Edward, 'and they haven't the faintest idea that they were entitled to a bigger one. They're not worrying and if they suddenly get their due proportion of that hundred thousand pounds, they'll be tickled to death.'

'Not as tickled as they would be if they had their due proportion of, say, two hundred thousand pounds, if that was the full amount. Or half a million pounds, if that was.'

'You can't have everything in this life,' said Edward. 'But it seems to me that that's getting a large proportion of everything. Perhaps I'd better go on to explain that the excess over a hundred thousand pounds was given away. There are obvious difficulties about getting it back. If the amount which can't be got back was comparatively small, the person concerned would probably pay it out of his own pocket, but, if it was very large, he wouldn't be able to do so. I can assure you of this. A hundred thousand pounds was all he had left after he had got rid of the rest.'

'I suppose it comes to this,' said Mr McManus. 'You did this for a friend, now he's in a spot and you're trying to get him out of it.'

'I've already said that I do not admit having done anything myself, but I agree that what I am doing now is for a friend. How are we going to leave it then?'

'I shall have to make a full report and put it before the Board at once.'

'Of course. But will you make it plain to them that, if you want further help from me it must be on the terms that they do not at the moment hand this matter over to the police.'

'How long will you be staying in Birmingham?'

'For as long as necessary to clear up this business as far as it can be cleared up at the moment.'

'Is there any chance of your producing the equipment which enabled this fraud to be perpetrated for our next meeting?'

'No, I'm afraid not,' said Edward. 'I will only do that when the whole matter is settled and I am quite prepared to make settlement conditional upon my doing it.'

'All right,' said Mr McManus. 'I'll get in touch with you at your hotel as soon as possible. Please let me know if you're going to move.'

'Are you proposing to have me watched?'

'Would you have any objection?'

'Not at the moment, but I should not be at all pleased if I were followed when I left Birmingham.'

Within an hour of Edward leaving Mr McManus the directors of Vulgans went into the matter very seriously at a Board

Meeting which had been specially convened. Mr McManus attended.

'It is pretty obvious to me, sir,' he said, addressing the chairman, 'that this man Livermore is the man who did this. But he's no fool. He said nothing to me which could possibly amount to an admission that he's guilty. Why he's doing this and why he did it originally I've no idea. But having regard to his previous convictions which I don't doubt, he has got some motive for his conduct.'

'Don't you think we ought to go to the police straightaway?' asked the chairman. 'It's really a matter for them.'

'If we do that at this stage, he says he won't help us any more. He's under no obligation to help the police and at the moment there is nothing whatever with which we can charge him.'

'You've no idea who else is involved?'

'No, but it might be possible to find out by investigating all large wins in the last two years, but this will take a considerable time and, if the parties concerned refuse to talk, we shall still have no evidence against anyone. But, on the other hand, he has said that, if we hold our hand, there is a possibility that the whole of the remaining prize money or at any rate the greater part of it may be repaid to us. Personally, sir, I should have thought that was worth waiting for. You see, it is not as though we have only his word for it. We have received a hundred thousand pounds in cash and that most certainly is a sign of good faith, if that's an appropriate term to use for people who've swindled you.'

'But suppose,' said the chairman, 'that we do get it all back? Are we going to let it go at that? Our great success rests upon the public's complete trust in us and, if people think that they can be diddled out of their prize money, not by any dishonesty on our part but by our failing to take enough steps to prevent fraud being practised, we shall lose that trust.'

'Surely, sir,' said Mr McManus, 'if we initiate a prosecution or if we give the police sufficient information to able them to do so, there will be the most tremendous publicity. This invention must be a fantastic one and the whole world will want to know about it. And why shouldn't some of our clients say to themselves, "Well, if it's happened this time, how many times has it happened before? How many big wins are on the level?" It seems to me, sir, with the greatest respect, that the last thing in the world we want is any publicity. If in fact the rest of the money is returned to us and we are given sufficient information to know the week in which it was obtained, we can then write to the people who got second, third, fourth and fifth dividends, send them an additional cheque and say that it has now transpired that there was a mistake and the first dividend was not in fact won, that the money has been returned and, in consequence, we have much pleasure in increasing the dividends in the following manner. The recipients will be absolutely delighted. At the very worst they will give information to the Press or to the broadcasting media and we shall be asked questions about it. All we have to say is that there was in fact a mistake, the wrong person was paid and, being an honest person, when the mistake was found out he has returned all the money. That will be the end of the matter. A very different state of affairs from the publicity which would be attached to a prosecution.'

'Do you trust this man?' asked the chairman.

'I don't know,' said Mr McManus. 'I don't at the moment distrust him, but of course he is an ex-criminal and there is no certainty in the matter. But I do ask myself why he should have had all that money sent to us and have come to me and have been pretty frank about it, if he weren't being reasonably honest on this occasion. So, sir, I would like the Board's authority to agree to the suggestion.'

'Very well then,' said the chairman. 'We will discuss the matter and let you know, but I may say that you have convinced me personally that, if we get all the money back, we should do nothing more about it.'

CHAPTER FOURTEEN

Remote Control

From the time Henry had restored relations with Douglas and Sheila he once again became a regular visitor, usually uninvited but welcome. Shortly after their dreadful discovery he came round before lunch one day in search of a drink.

'Not like the old days,' he said, 'when I started to wonder whether it was fair to touch you for a glass of sherry. Could I have one, by the way, please? Not British, if you don't mind.'

'There's something we've got to tell you,' said Douglas.

'Fire away. I'm all attention or I shall be when I've got the sherry. I find that, when I'm waiting for something to eat or drink, my mind is apt to concentrate on that aspect of the occasion and I can't really attend properly to anything else.'

'You'd like it dry, I take it?' said Douglas.

'Please.'

Douglas brought Henry his sherry and a glass for himself.

'Cheers.'

'It's not a very cheerful time for us.'

'I'm sorry to hear that. Illness of some kind? One of the girls?'

'No.'

'No kidnap threats or anything?'

'No. In fact,' went on Douglas, 'I think I can say that they will be most unlikely now.'

'That's good. What's troubling you? This is good sherry, by the way. It goes terribly well with those salted almonds you used to have.'

Douglas got up and went to the cupboard and produced the salted almonds. 'I should make the most of them,' he said. 'There won't be any more when they run out.'

'What on earth's happened? Have you been gambling on the Stock Exchange and lost it all?'

'We've had to give it back.'

'I can't believe it.'

'It's true. We've had to give back all that we've still got and I expect we shall have to try to get back some of the amounts we've given away if they haven't already been spent.'

'Why on earth?'

'I can't go into details, but it was paid to us by mistake.'

'But that's ridiculous. You had the eight draws and there was nobody else with them, so you scooped the pool.'

'That's what they thought at the time. In fact we haven't. We weren't entitled to any dividend at all. So naturally we've got to give it back.'

'This is incredible,' said Henry. 'I'm quite certain the pools companies take infinite trouble before they pay out their dividends, particularly a dividend of this kind. How on earth can such a mistake be made?'

'I can't go into that,' said Douglas, 'but we have no doubt whatever that we are both legally and morally liable to return the money.'

'But I thought these pool transactions were binding in honour only?'

'From our point of view it wouldn't make any difference if we were only morally liable to repay the money. We should have to repay whatever was left of it. But in point of fact we're legally liable as well. The situation is this. Pools companies are not legally liable to pay out the prizes to anybody, but if by mistake they pay out to the wrong person, that person is legally liable to pay back the money, certainly as long as he's got it. So, when the stocks give out, I'm afraid it's back to British sherry.'

'And the old bicycle and all that?' said Henry.

'Yes, I'm afraid so.'

'That will be terrible. It was bad enough before you won the money but, now you've got used to it and a reasonable standard of life when you can entertain your friends in a proper manner, it will be awful to have to go back to the old regime.'

'I hope you will still come and see us, Henry.'

'Oh, you can rely on me. I'm not just a fair-weather friend. You must admit I used to come to you when there were no such things as salted almonds – by jove, these are good – or a really decent sherry around. D'you know, I believe I'd come to you even if there were nothing around. Don't hold me to that. It's agin my nature. Mrs Mountjoy will be very upset. D'you want the new lawn-mower back?'

'I hadn't thought of that,' said Douglas.

'We'll try to manage without it. I hope you won't want the car.'

'At the moment everything's in the melting pot. We don't quite know what's going to happen.'

'I'm terribly sorry,' said Henry. 'Lucky you didn't give up your job, though.'

'I never thought of giving it up. No, when we've cleared up the mess, probably we'll have to go back to living just as we used to. It will be a bit hard at first, but we'll soon get used to it. I must admit I'll be glad when we have cleared it all up. You see, we gave away four hundred thousand pounds and it's the wretched people who have still got it that I'm afraid will have to hand it back. Of course if I had the money myself we wouldn't dream of allowing them to do so, but we haven't. After we've given up all we've got left, we'll have nothing whatever to spare. I'm afraid that some of the charities to whom we gave large amounts aren't going to be at all pleased. Our solicitor says that, if they've spent the money, they'll be all right.'

'Get on to them quick and tell them to spend it,' said Henry.

At that moment Theo came in.

'If you could forget your sherry for a moment, would you mind coming out here?'

'I'll finish it first,' said Henry. 'Will it run to another when I come back?' he asked Douglas.

'At the moment,' said Douglas, 'it will.'

They went out with Theo towards the workshop. When they had gone some way down the path leading to it, they saw that there was some white paint on it. It had obviously been put on some days previously as it had already collected a little dirt on it.

From the time the fraud had been discovered Theo had done everything he could not only to speed up his new invention but to speed up the marketing of it. He had compared it with cats'-eyes and it was a fair comparison. His idea was a simple one to think of but it required a very considerable technological advance to make it workable. He was undoubtedly right in thinking that, if he could perfect it, he would make a fortune.

It was a thing which he had thought about from his schooldays. While cycling down a long, dangerous lane in which the local authority had tried to mitigate the danger by having white lines at all the bends, he narrowly avoided hitting a workman who was engaged in repainting part of a white line. He fell off his bicycle but was not badly hurt. As he rode thoughtfully back to school it seemed to him extraordinary that towards the end of the 20th century when men could go to the moon, when a man speaking in London could be heard quite clearly in Australia through the use of satellites, when broadcast programmes could be stored in those satellites and released at will, when nuclear power was available to destroy the world or to make it very comfortable, that hundreds, if not thousands, of men up and down the country should be engaged in repainting white lines manually. How absurd it was that so many men were employed on what was such simple work.

As he grew older he began to wonder if in some way the process could be mechanised. Later on, when he began to play about with wireless, ideas started to come to him and it was from this idea that he developed a transmitter which could control the action of radioactive ink. Would it not be possible, in a similar way, to control the white lines on the roads? He found this a much more difficult proposition, because in effect what the radio waves had to do was to get rid of the accumulations of dirt which gradually obliterated the white lines. But within the last months he thought that he had invented a method by which by impregnating the white paint with radioactive matter it might be possible by the use of a transmitter to renew the white lines until the paint ceased to be radioactive. This should cover a period of several years, at least two or three. It should also be possible to build a very large transmitter which would cover many square miles of white lines. Although the cost of transmitters necessary to cover the whole of the British Isles would be considerable, the probability was that in the end a very substantial saving could be made in the cost of maintaining white lines. He had tested his invention in a small way and it appeared to work, but it would be necessary to try it on the actual white lines themselves and it would take at least a month to demonstrate that the invention worked satisfactorily.

In view of the shortage of time Theo acted sooner than he otherwise would have done. He went to see the county surveyor and asked him whether he would be prepared to take part in a small experiment covering a few hundred yards of white lines. The county surveyor was naturally sceptical, but, on having the ink removal invention demonstrated to him, he realised that there might be much more in the idea than he had at first thought. And, if there were, he would be quite pleased to be associated with the first use of it in the country. So he agreed to Theo treating enough paint to cover a few hundred yards of white lines in the neighbourhood with radioactive material. Normally, he said, the lines had to be renewed every three or four months, but he thought there would be sufficient deterioration in the white lines in a month to be just worth while. So Theo was allowed to impregnate enough white paint for the test to be made and he personally followed the white paint to see that it was that paint which was put upon the road and not by accident some unimpregnated paint. After he had done this there was nothing he could do but wait.

It was on the day when he learned that the test had been entirely successful that he invited his father and Henry out into the garden.

'Now, just watch that paint while I go into the workshop. Tell me what you see.'

Theo went into the workshop and they watched the paint. At first they noticed nothing and then suddenly Henry said : 'Isn't it getting whiter?'

'It is, you know,' said Douglas. 'I'm sure it is. Yes, look there.'

Theo came out of the workshop. 'Well?' he asked.

'It definitely got brighter,' said his father.

'How on earth did you do it?' asked Henry.

'It's an extension of that ink trick that I showed you at that party some time ago.'

'But if you can do it here, can you do it on the roads? I imagine you can.'

'Certainly.'

'So they won't have to go on painting white lines? You can do it all with your invention? '

'That's the idea,' said Theo.

'You'll be a millionaire,' said Henry.

'Half a million will do,' said Theo.